Three's A Crowd

A Patrick Shea Mystery

By Mary Lydon Simonsen

Quail Creek Publishing LLC

http://marysimonsenfanfiction.blogspot.com

Printed in the United States of America
Published by Quail Creek Publishing, LLC
Peoria, Arizona
quailcreekpub@hotmail.com
www.marysimonsenfanfiction.blogspot.com

ISBN: 978-061565337-2

©2012 Quail Creek Publishing LLC

Cover art: I-Stock Photo #15050699

Note from the Author

Three's A Crowd is a novella introducing the character of Patrick Shea, a Detective Sergeant serving in a Criminal Investigation Department (CID) in London's Metropolitan Police, a copper who hopes to be assigned to a murder investigation team at New Scotland Yard. In the story, the police stations of Renwick and Hampden are fictional, and their locations within Greater London are deliberately ambiguous. All incidents and characters are also fictional. Although some locations in London and names mentioned are real, they have been added only for the purpose of providing an aura of authenticity. Any similarity to real persons, living or dead, is purely coincidental and is not intended by the author.

The reader will find a glossary of British terms at the end of the book, but it may be helpful for you to be familiar with the ranks of the Metropolitan Police in London: police constable (PC), detective constable (DC), sergeant, detective sergeant (DS), detective inspector (DI), detective chief inspector (DCI), superintendent, chief superintendent, commander, deputy assistant commissioner, assistant commissioner, deputy commissioner, and commissioner.

For more information on the Patrick Shea mystery series, please visit my Facebook page: Patrick Shea Mysteries.

Prologue

She was alone, or nearly alone, on Old School Road, the ancient trees crowding out the light from the street lamps and muffling the sounds from the nearby motorway. Despite the quiet, she was struggling to hear the message on her mobile when, suddenly, from behind, someone was tearing off her hat and yanking her head back by her hair. With the mugger's forearm pressed against her throat, she could not call out. As she clawed desperately at the arm around her neck, her assailant landed a hard punch to the side of her head. After releasing her, she fell against a brick wall before dropping to her knees. Down on all fours, fighting for breath, she heard someone shouting, and a second person appeared out of the shadows. After ringing 999, her saviour tried to help her stand up, but overcome by a wave of nausea, she felt herself falling through space, away from the barking dog and the man's voice, and she was convinced that these were to be the last sounds she would hear before she died.

.

Chapter 1

Autumn 2003

While Detective Sergeant Patrick Shea blew on his hands, his partner sipped coffee from the lid of her Thermos. It wasn't a particularly cold night, but sitting in an unmarked police car for two hours resulted in chills and tight muscles and the reason why Patrick was jiggling his left leg. But he wasn't going to complain about the chill as a blast of Arctic air, by way of Greenland, was scheduled to arrive the following day, signalling the start of another long, gray winter.

"Honestly, what are the chances of us catching this bloke?" Detective Constable Molly Updike asked while trying to scratch an itch under her stab vest. "How do we know where he's going to strike next? Even if he obliges us by staying in Hampden, it's still a lot of territory to cover."

"We are here because Superintendent Craig said that this is where the burglar will strike, and you know the super is never wrong."

"Two miles from here, no one would give a toss

about five burglaries in five months," Molly said, pointing her coffee cup in a westerly direction. "Instead, they'd be celebrating. It's only because this neighbourhood is full of nobs that the overtime and manpower were approved."

"You're catching on, Molly," Patrick said to the newest member of the Hampden nick, a lady who had been in a sour mood for days.

Afraid of the answer he might receive, female complaints and all, he opted not to enquire about the cause of her unhappiness. It was better just to humour her.

"Remember it's nobs who write letters to the newspapers and to their representatives in Parliament and who show up at Council meetings. Unlike the lot who live about two miles from here," he said, gesturing in the direction of the South Hill estate, the site of two rundown high-rise buildings, straddling the boundaries of the Hampden and Renwick police stations, "they also happen to vote."

Molly sipped more coffee. They had to be sips. Unlike Patrick, she couldn't make use of the nearest bush to relieve herself.

"But it was you and not Craig who figured out the burglar's MO," Molly said, continuing to press.

"Elementary, my dear Updike," Patrick answered, punting the compliment. As the newest DS at the Hampden station, he thought it best to keep his head down and let others have the credit. He had received this sage advice from his Uncle Brendan, a copper with the Metropolitan police for thirty years who had retired as a detective chief inspector. "The burglar strikes when there's a half moon—enough light to get around, but not so much that he glows in the dark. And he knows who has real security and not just some decal stuck in their window. He also knows when the residents will be away from home. In other words, he does his homework."

"But why this street?"

Molly had been late for the briefing—again—and had caught only the tail end of Craig's address to his troops, the one where he exhorted his coppers to go out and "nab the blackguard." Although Patrick had tried to cover for his partner, Craig had noted her absence. If they nicked the burglar, probably nothing would be said. But if they didn't, her tardiness would be reflected in her six-month performance review, and Craig would let her know about it.

Superintendent Craig was the perfect example of a 21st Century copper: someone who scored well on exams, was analytical, looked like a proper policeman in his uniform, and photographed well for the newspapers. Additionally, he understood all the latest technology, a computer whiz who knew how to analyse data and make it work for the officers under his command. The map he had put up at the briefing showed a logical progression in the break-ins that were upsetting Hampden's wealthier homeowners. If the pattern continued, the thief would burgle a house on one of three streets, and there were stakeouts on the other two as well. Craig's major failing was his personality or lack of it. No one actually disliked Superintendent Craig. It was his lack of passion and an inability to rally his officers under his leadership that had senior detectives serving *under* him wondering how he had ended up getting promoted *over* them.

"Word in the canteen is that you really cleaned up on Friday at Dillon's house," Molly said in an attempt to keep the conversation going so she wouldn't nod off.

Patrick smiled at the memory of his raking in one pot after another. "Honest to God, I couldn't lose. Straights, flushes, full houses, one after the other. Unbelievable! Best night I've had in a long time. I raked in more than sixty quid."

"You know what they say: 'Lucky in cards...'"

"Yeah, yeah, yeah," he said, and then told his partner he had to water the shrubs. But when he got back in the car, Molly picked up where she had left off.

"How's it going with the girlfriend?"

With of his good looks, killer smile, and a way with the ladies, Patrick was teased unmercifully by his fellow coppers, but his partner knew he was a one-woman man—at least one woman at a time.

"She's not my girlfriend," Patrick answered while scanning the street. "Susan is someone I see occasionally."

"Do you have a change of clothes at her flat?"

"Yeah. Why?"

"Then she's your girlfriend. Those are the rules. You get a drawer in her bedroom and two feet of cupboard space, and she gets to call you her boyfriend."

Patrick didn't respond. That was a woman's point of view. And the only reason he had left his clothes at Susan's was because his brother had moved into his flat. Although Patrick was hardly a zealot in keeping his place neat, Jack Shea made his older brother look like Mr. Clean. Patrick could get past the clutter. It was the dirty plates in the sink, overflowing rubbish bin, and hair in the drain that ticked him off. And because his brother was a slob, he had started staying overnight at Susan's. He now knew that had been a mistake.

The morning after that first overnight, Susan had risen at the crack of dawn to make eggs and waffles before Patrick went off to work. But there was a price to be paid for clean sheets and a hot breakfast. After finishing the last of the waffles, Susan had asked him what time he would be *home* for dinner. He had tried to explain that a junior detective in a Criminal

Investigation Department rarely knew when he would walk in the door, and after a long day, he would probably crash at his own flat. He had escaped her noose—that time at least—but he could feel it tightening nonetheless.

"Don't get me wrong. I like Susan," Patrick finally answered his partner, "but it's not going to lead to a jewellery store where we pick out matching rings. I've already done the long walk down the aisle, and it lasted all of three years."

Patrick thought about Allison, his ex-wife and mother of his eight-year-old son. They had met while he was attending City University and had married as soon as Patrick had graduated with a degree in criminology. During her final year at the University of London, Ally had found out she was pregnant, and her plans to become a psychologist came to a screeching halt. During their marriage, she had worked as a teacher at a nursery school chasing after toddlers, including their son, teaching them to recognise their colours and shapes—hardly the satisfying career she had been hoping for. The pressures of being married to a uniformed cop in a dodgy neighbourhood didn't help matters. Resentment ensued; divorce followed. Although theirs was an amicable parting and they shared joint custody of their son, Patrick disliked failure, and was there a bigger personal failure than the woman you loved walking out on you? If he ever entertained the idea of taking a second leap into the marriage pool, the woman would have to be one hell of a gal in order to get him to utter the words "I do" again. In that regard, Susan didn't even come close.

"May I play the role of Agony Aunt?" Molly asked.

"Do I have a choice?" he asked, jiggling the door handle, pretending to attempt an escape.

"You've been with Susan as long as I've been at Hampden. Although it's only four months, I feel like I've been here forever. I'm sure Susan feels the same way about you."

"I think I've just been insulted."

"You know what I mean," she said, punching him in the arm. "After a woman's been with a man for three months, she starts looking at bridal magazines. She can't help herself. My advice to you is if you don't think it's going to work out, call it quits now. Otherwise, you are setting yourself up for a messy break-up."

"Actually, I've been dropping hints that it's not going to work. And I don't anticipate a messy break-up. Susan is not a drama queen. She's more of a... Holy shit! There he is! Jesus, he just put on a balaclava," Patrick said as he felt a rush of adrenalin. "Molly, notify the other units and wait for back-up." He quietly slipped out of the car.

Armed with an expandable baton, Patrick inched

his way into the yard, silently thanking the intruder for leaving the wrought-iron gate open. He quickly made his way to the rear of the house just in time to see the burglar working the lock. Even though it looked like an easy collar, Patrick would wait for backup. There would be no heroics.

By the time the man had finished pilfering the jewellery and enjoying a glass of wine—his signature for each burglary—four coppers were standing behind Patrick waiting for the thief to come out. After assessing the situation, the burglar surrendered without a fight, but not before handing Patrick a red rose nicked from a vase on the dining-room table.

"Christ, you're a lucky sod, Shea," DS Prentiss said, putting his arm around Patrick's shoulders. "You tell him to drop the bag, and he just does it. Why do I always get the ones who come out swinging? Last month, I took a bag of silver plate right in the mouth from a thieving bastard."

"That's because you're ugly, and a punch in the face won't make any difference to you," Patrick said, smiling. However, he nodded in acknowledgement that this was one of the easiest arrests he had ever made.

"And he gave you a flower. Must have got a look-see at your baby blues before you cuffed him. Instantly smitten, he was," DC Dillon added, and Patrick knew he was in for it once he got back to the station.

"The price I pay for being so good-looking," he said while passing the rose to a woman police constable.

"You may have got the collar, but at least I won't have to sit in the nick for the next four hours processing the bastard and doing the paperwork," Prentiss continued, "to say nothing of getting all dressed up for your court appearance."

"Too right," Patrick said, thinking about the reams of paper he already had stacked on his desk requiring his attention and the hours he would spend waiting in hallways before being called to testify in court.

Two hours later, after processing the burglar, Patrick was finished, and he had to decide if he should head for his own flat or Susan's. What it came down to was a choice between sleeping in a warm, comfy bed versus Susan's growing need to hear words of endearment. He opted for his flat.

* * *

"I didn't think you'd be coming home tonight," Patrick's younger brother said while picking his dirty clothes off the floor under the pull-out sofa bed, sweeping up fast-food wrappers as he went. A year earlier, Jack Shea had been arrested for possession of cannabis for personal use. As a first-time offender, he had been given an order of supervision and a £250 fine before being released into his brother's custody. The supervisory period was nearly at an end, and it was Patrick's intention to reintroduce the youngest Shea into the bosom of his family in Kilburn as soon as the clock struck midnight.

"You still on with Susan?" Jack asked, hoping it would distract his brother from the empty pizza box and crushed Coke can poking out from under the bed.

"Not really," Patrick answered after taking a beer from the fridge. Before sitting down, he placed a throw his mother had crocheted over a chair to protect his shirt and wondered how two such different people could have been spawned by the same parents.

"What happened with Susan?" Jack asked, popping the tab on his own brew.

Having consumed a year's supply of his brother's beer, he made a mental note to buy Patrick a six pack before going back to his parents' house. Although he wasn't looking forward to coming under the aegis of Daniel and Fiona Shea once again, he recognised the signs that Patrick was experiencing fraternal fatigue, especially when Jack had his girlfriend with him, someone who could get under his brother's skin without her even opening her mouth.

"The complaints began," Patrick said, thinking of the last spat he had had with Susan. "You know the bit about how we don't spend enough time together, and when we do, I've got Josh with me. Both true. So we're arguing a lot. But what am I supposed to do? I'm his dad."

Patrick's gaze shifted to the picture of his son on the end table, and he smiled. He had seen Josh over the weekend at a football match at St. Edmund's, the tuition paid by Ally's husband of three years, Dr. Peter Petrie. If he had put an advertisement in *The Times* for a stand-up guy to be his son's stepfather, he couldn't have done better than good old Peter, a total nerd, but nerds made good dads. An added benefit was that Peter was an orthodontist as Josh definitely was going to need braces. Although athletically challenged himself, Peter had recognised that Josh was a naturally gifted athlete and was taking the boy to the French Alps for his first ever skiing trip, a holiday well beyond the means of a London copper.

But Patrick's job and son weren't the only points of contention with Susan. Her major beef was a lack of any discussion concerning a future together. Molly had been right about the bridal magazine. He had seen an issue with the address label of the tanning salon where she worked edging out from under her side of the bed and had given it a good kick. It was Susan's opinion that, after four months, they should at least be living together—an idea he refused to entertain. He had never even moved in with his previous girlfriend, Annie Jameson, and they had been together for more than a year. But then that had been Annie's idea. In her mind, it would be less stressful dating someone who worked in such a dangerous occupation if they lived apart. In that way, she wouldn't be staring at the door every night waiting for him to come home. Annie's preference was for him to ring her shortly before he left the station, and they would go from there.

"At least Susan's not like Mad Marta," Jack added.

Patrick shuddered at the thought of a woman he had been with exactly two times. He had met Marta Bledsloe at a dance club and had actually believed her when she said she was a party girl who wasn't interested in anything serious. Since it had been several months since his breakup with Annie, and being horny as hell, he had decided it was time to get back into the game. After leaving the club, he had stopped by a chemist's shop to pick up a pack of condoms.

When they got back to her place, she had displayed a remarkable agility in an all-night sex romp. But after the third go-round, Patrick grew tired of the gymnastics and just wanted to go to sleep. On their first and only date, they never made it out of her flat. In that short acquaintance, he had noted Marta's need for constant contact, demonstrated by her running her hands up and down his back or resting her fingers inside his jeans. But those quirks were mere annoyances when compared to her habit of tracing the outline of his face with her tongue on its way to its final destination—his ears. On the way out the door, he had told her it had been fun and for her to take care of herself.

Soon thereafter, he had met Susan Corning. After Marta's in-the-sack athletics, he found Susan to be refreshingly boring. A little foreplay to get things going, some heavy breathing and heaving, and they were done, a definite plus for a copper who worked long hours, and her mattress was really comfortable. But even before he had slept with Susan, he had made it clear that his son was his top priority, followed closely by the job. On those days when he had Josh, he never stayed overnight at her flat. According to Susan, his failure to share her bed in front of his son showed a lack of trust on his part. What she actually meant was a lack of commitment, but if that was the way she felt about it, so be it. He didn't want his kid to think his relationship with Susan was more than it was.

Then there was the job. Being a detective was the only thing Patrick had ever wanted to do, and when he had been a uniformed cop patrolling a beat, he couldn't wait to get into CID. Although he had heard the Criminal Investigation Department was a bottomless pit of paperwork, long hours, and erratic schedules, the reality was much worse. But if he kept plugging away, working the cases and doing the legwork, he had a decent chance of ending up at New Scotland Yard on a murder investigation team. He had already had an interview with Superintendent Craig, and it had gone well—at least that was his take on it.

"Did you record Dr. Who?" Patrick asked his brother. After Jack nodded, Patrick indicated there would be no more talk of girlfriends. As far as he was concerned, nabbing a burglar was easier than trying to figure out how to make a woman happy.

Chapter 2

As a way of celebrating his collar, on the morning after nicking the Hampden Burglar, Patrick arrived at the station carrying a box of donuts from Krispy Kreme, an American chain that had opened a shop around the corner from the station. Apparently, coppers eating Danish pastries and donuts crossed international boundaries, and the franchise was thriving.

After placing the box near the coffee pot, he stopped at Gwen Evans' desk to pick up any messages that hadn't landed in his voice mail. Although only in her late forties, Gwen was called "Mum" by all the detectives because she covered their backs with the super. She was also a good listener, and most of the coppers in the station had bent her ear at one time or another about a personal problem or the job.

Patrick was one of Gwen's favourites. She knew his work ethic and determination to end up on a murder investigation team at New Scotland Yard had cost him his marriage and was probably the cause of his breakup with the only serious girlfriend he had

had since his divorce. Knowing he was unhappy with his current romantic interest, and in order to save him from becoming just another lonely copper sitting in a pub staring into a pint at the end of a shift, she was determined to find him a girlfriend, passing out his picture to prospective dates as if she was an in-house dating service. It was Gwen who had provided him with his date for the annual station gala.

Gwen, who had been on a diet as long as Patrick had been at the Hampden nick, tapped her bulging middle as a way of declining an offered donut, but then held up a copy of *Global News*, informing him that he was in today's newspaper.

"I'm in that rag? Why?" *Global News* was a tabloid specialising in sex and gore from around the world. None of his recent cases met their macabre criteria.

"You're the copper who nicked the Hampden Burglar," she said, opening the paper and pointing to his name in the weekly "On the Beat" column. "They intend to do a longer story on you over the weekend."

"Where did they get my picture?"

"They have every copper's picture on file just in case one of them becomes a star like you." *Or gets wounded or killed*, Patrick thought. "And they want to conduct a phone interview with you at three o'clock tomorrow afternoon arranged personally by His Highness. You know how Superintendent Craig loves liaising with the media."

"A phone interview? For what? This is a load of shite," Patrick said. When something irked him, the Irish phrasing of his parents came through. "As soon as the burglar saw all the coppers waiting for him, he surrendered. I happened to be the first one he saw."

"You're being modest, Patrick."

"No, I'm not. Ask anyone. Most particularly ask Dillon or Prentiss," he said, pointing to the two detectives. "They'll tell you what went down. It's the easiest arrest I've ever made. He would have surrendered to my gran if she had been standing there."

"This kind of thing looks good in your file," Gwen whispered. "Besides, the only thing the public likes better than a hero is a good-looking one, and you fit the bill."

"You're right. I am a good-looking lad," Patrick said, resigned to his fate. "I'd better get on with it. I see DC Updike is already hard at work," and he walked toward his partner. "What's with all the flowers?" Patrick asked, picking a red carnation out of a vase on her desk. "You and Eddie have a fight?"

"No, Eddie and me did not have a fight," Molly said with way too much emphasis, but if they had, she would probably win. She was a stocky blonde with a low centre of gravity and had been a star in her self-defence class with a tendency to go for the eyes. He wouldn't want to tussle with her, and he considered himself to be in good shape. "But I'm not the only one who got them," Molly said, pointing with her chin to an identical vase on Patrick's desk.

"Oh, I get it," Patrick said, turning around to look at his fellow coppers. "It's my mates' way of congratulating me—and you—on a job well done in catching the Hampden Burglar," Patrick said in a voice loud enough for everyone in the room to hear. After plucking a flower from the vase and putting it between his teeth, he performed an abbreviated flamenco dance to the roar of laughter and a round of applause. After breaking off most of the stem, he put it behind Dillon's ear.

"Bollocks!" Molly shot back after Patrick had finished. "They're having a laugh at your expense— and mine as well."

"I know, Molly. It's a joke. I was expecting something like this after the Hampden Burglar presented me with a red rose he nicked from the house."

"What's wrong with landing an easy one every now and then?" Molly said, addressing her fellow coppers. "We were in that bloody car for more than two hours. We did the legwork. We earned it."

"Arsework, you mean," DS Prentiss said, and the room again erupted in laughter.

"Fancy a cup of tea, Molly?" Patrick asked, and

he walked with his partner to the canteen.

After securing two teas, Patrick got after it. "Molly, you've been a copper long enough to know that if you can't take a joke, you become the joke."

Molly stared into her cup. "I wouldn't mind it so much if the shit was more evenly spread out. But I'm tired of all the 'Updick' or 'Are you a dyke,' comments. And why are most of the jokes on us along with all the crap assignments?"

"Come on, Molly. Think back to the time when you first became a copper. It was all about puking drunks or dealing with smart-arse gang members, that is, when you weren't on rubbish trawls, climbing in skips, or knocking on doors until your knuckles were raw. You know shit rolls downhill. What you have to do is climb to the top of the hill so you can get out of the waste stream." Molly said nothing. "You know, I don't think this has much to do with some juvenile kidding by your peers. What's going on?"

"It's Eddie," Molly said, speaking of her husband of eight years. "We met when we were both probationary constables. We knew it would be difficult with both of us being cops and both wanting to become detectives, but we agreed to support whoever made detective constable first. But that's not how it's working out. Because he's still in uniform and works regular hours, Eddie tells me that because of all the hours I put in here that he's *babysitting*

Colin all the time and that I'm only a part-time parent. Patrick, you don't babysit your own kid. You raise him. You parent him. But you don't *babysit* him."

"I agree it's a poor choice of words," Patrick said, recalling a similar conversation with Ally, "but men aren't known for their verbal skills. To Eddie, babysitting is the same as spending time with his kid."

"Honestly, I don't know if it's possible for a husband and wife with a kid to be coppers," Molly said, shaking her head. "We're fighting like cats and dogs over who should be doing what. Because Eddie absolutely hates dropping Colin off at nursery school, I've been doing it and that's the reason I was late for the briefing. And with everything that's going on, Eddie's talking about a second kid. Where the hell did that come from? We're already on a tight budget. I think he wants to get me pregnant so I'll stay home."

Patrick felt bad for Molly, but she was right. It was hard enough on a relationship when only one of the parties was a copper—next to impossible when two cops tied the knot. Add kids and the marriage either fell apart or one of them changed careers. All the evidence he needed was right there in his own station. The divorce rate among police officers was well above the national average, and he was one of the statistics. Another reason to keep his life simple and stay single, he reminded himself.

"Oh, enough with the pity party," Molly said after a prolonged silence. "As for our fellow officers, I can take a joke. I *will* take a joke. No more pouting. So what's up with our burglar?"

After returning to the nick with the Hampden Burglar, Patrick had sent Molly home. There was no point in both of them hanging around while waiting for the paperwork to make its way through the labyrinth of a police station.

"His name is Tommy Jacobs, an unemployed house painter who likes to listen to classical music and enjoy a glass of wine while savouring his loot, and someone whose father just happens to be a locksmith. While I was booking him, Jacobs explained that he only took what he needed to pay his rent for that month, which accounts for the frequency of the burglaries, and he pointed out all the good stuff he left behind that he could have nicked. He also mentioned that he never left a mess for the owners. I have to admit he's the neatest thief I've ever arrested. And I really appreciated the confession. No court date, and it saves so much time."

"And I suppose Mr. Jacobs hopes that his leaving a tidy scene will be a reason for mitigation?" Patrick nodded. "Does he have any idea how creepy it is to know that some pervert has been in your home rummaging through your stuff?"

A year earlier, Molly's sister had been burgled.

Fearing that a stranger had touched her knickers, she had emptied her underwear drawer into a bin bag and walked it out to the dustbin. The sense of being personally violated was a common reaction by those whose homes had been burgled even though they had not been present when the thief was in the house. In some cases, the residents couldn't get past the incident and ended up moving out.

"In my opinion, the Hampden Burglar considers himself to be in the Cary Grant category—a second-story man, someone who looks good in a tuxedo." There was a blank expression from Molly. "You know, Cary Grant and Grace Kelly in *To Catch a Thief*, French Riviera, Monaco, sports cars."

"You watch Cary Grant movies?"

"We're talking classics here."

Molly shook her head. "No wonder you have trouble getting dates."

Chapter 3

Through good policing, hard work, high exam scores, and the Metropolitan Police's fast-tracking program, to say nothing of the luck of the Irish, Patrick Shea had landed in the Hampden CID as a detective sergeant after serving as a uniformed copper and detective constable at Renwick. Renwick, a largely blue-collar borough that had seen an uptick in crime mostly due to a spill-over of the drug trade from other boroughs, had been a good station where a young copper could cut his teeth. In upscale Hampden, the only serious crime occurred in an area bordering Renwick that included a few streets of low-income terrace houses that had yet to be gentrified and the derelict South Hill estate that was separated from Hampden proper by a brick wall and a busy road. The Hampden Council had dealt with the problem of South Hill by condemning it, but the actual demolition was still months, if not years, down the road.

Despite his promotion and move to a CID in a station considered to be a cushy assignment, his poker mates were the uniformed cops he had served with at the Renwick station, including Sergeant John Stanley, who was now making his way toward Patrick's desk.

"Good to see you, John," Patrick said while shaking the man's hand, but he wasn't sure if he meant it. It was Stanley who had handled the arrest of his kid brother and the reason why Jack had avoided doing jail time for possession. Had Jack done something to prompt Stanley's visit?

"Have you got time for lunch, Patrick?"

Patrick nodded and headed back to the canteen. After grabbing packaged sandwiches and salads, the two men found seats away from the buzz of their fellow officers who were talking about everything from recent arrests to the football club they supported as well as the news that Mick Jagger of the Rolling Stones was to be knighted by Prince Charles. The consensus was that a true anti-establishment rocker would have declined the title. Apparently, Keith Richards was not happy with his band mate.

A polar opposite to Superintendent Craig, Sergeant John Stanley practiced policing by following his gut, not computer printouts. Before assuming the operational command position of sergeant, the officer responsible for supervising constables, his gut had led to an impressive number of arrests, and he had the awards to prove it. While at Renwick, whenever he hit a brick wall, John was Patrick's first stop for advice.

"Last time we spoke, you were thinking about sitting for the detective's exam," Patrick said.

"Nah," Stanley responded, shaking his head. "I decided to give it a pass. I've seen what the schedules and hours in CID can do to a marriage. Ruth and the kids are more important to me than being a detective. Besides, I like working with uniformed coppers. It keeps me closer to the street, and that's what I want. If anything is fixable, it has to be done in the neighbourhoods by coppers who know their patch. For me it's personal. I live in the neighbourhood where I work. Renwick is a nice place to live for a working man, and I want to keep it that way."

Patrick immediately thought about Eddie Updike, Molly's husband, and his desire to get out of uniform and wondered if Stanley might have a talk with him. The biggest advantage to being in uniform was a regular schedule that allowed for a copper to make plans with his family. In CID, you were expected to get the job done no matter how long it took, especially if you had designs on a position with a murder investigation team.

"No doubt CID can be a marriage killer," Patrick said, thinking of all the hours he put in with nothing extra showing up in his pay packet, "and that's why I got a divorce before becoming a detective constable at Renwick. Got that out of the way."

"Cheeky bastard," Stanley said, chuckling.

After catching up on the latest news out of the Renwick station, Patrick finally got after it. "Is this about my brother?"

"No. Sorry, Patrick. Didn't mean to give you that impression. From what I hear, Jack's been toeing the line. Not hanging about with the blokes what got him into trouble in the first place. No, nothing wrong there. But I do have some bad news." Stanley took a deep breath before continuing. "I know you and Annie Jameson were a couple for quite a while..."

At the sound of Annie's name, Patrick felt his chest tighten. After his divorce from Allison, he thought he would never again fall in love, but that was before he had laid eyes on Annie Jameson, an intelligent, witty, petite brunette with dark eyes and curves in all the right places. Annie shared his interest in classic movies, football, Monty Python, and Dr. Who and was someone who was a good fit with his large and loud Irish-Catholic family. Even better, his son thought she was "cool." But the relationship had ended when she had confessed to a "sexual indiscretion." Although the breakup had taken place a year earlier, the wound had not completely healed.

"Assaulted, she was, on her way home on Old School Road."

"Is she... Is she going to be okay?"

"She's in hospital with a concussion, but it looks like she'll be all right."

"Anything else?"

"No. No sexual assault if that's what you mean."

"Why don't you run it down for me?"

After finishing a bite of his sandwich, Stanley summarised the assault. "On Tuesday night, Annie was leaving the library at Roehampton University at about 10:00. While walking down Old School Road, she was attacked from behind, and her assailant put her in a chokehold. After punching her in the head, Annie was pushed into a wrought-iron railing. On the way down, she hit her head against a low brick wall supporting the railings and was knocked out."

"Witnesses?"

"No motor traffic on the street, or none Annie can recall, and all the houses on that section of Old School sit way back behind ten-foot hedges, so none of the residents saw or heard anything. Fortunately, a bloke was out walking his dog and raised the alarm, and her attacker took off."

"Description of the assailant?"

"Nothing from Annie. She never saw him. And not much from the dog walker either. All he could give us was that the bloke was wearing a dark anorak and jeans and that he had a slight build with skinny legs. Our witness thought he must be a runner as he was down the street and onto the heath before he could phone the police. Not a whole lot to go on. I sent a copy of the report to you by e-mail. It will answer most of your questions, that is, before you go and have a talk with Annie yourself."

Patrick shook his head. His breakup with Annie had been particularly ugly. While he had been making plans to ask her to marry him, Annie had been enjoying a sexual romp. Completely blindsided by her admission, he had basically showed her the door, telling her he never wanted to see her again. Until a month ago, he had got his wish. Following an awkward exchange of pleasantries at a cashpoint machine, they had wished each other well and went on their way. Two weeks later, they reprised their meeting in the frozen-food aisle at Tesco's, and the conversation, although short, was easy. That's what he liked best about Annie. When he was with her, he never had to work at it.

"Well, that's up to you, but I know where I'd put my money," Stanley said, rising. "I'm sure you have more questions, but I've got to get back. I used up most of my lunch hour coming over here. Traffic is a nightmare, and the only parking space available was marked 'disabled badge holders only,' but I took it anyway. I hope I don't get a ticket," he said with a chuckle. Patrick stood up and shook Stanley's hand. "While reading the file, keep in mind it was written by a police cadet who needs to spend a little more time studying her crime classifications. But you'll spot the mistake right away. If you've got any questions, give me a ring or come by the house. Ruth would love to see you."

"I appreciate your coming over. It would have been a hard thing to hear on the phone or find out through the grapevine."

"You'd have done the same," Stanley said. "Oh, by the way, I ran into Bernadette at the market. Your sister told me to tell you that you're overdue for a visit to your mum's."

"Yeah, I need to get over there, and I will, just as soon as Jack's off probation. I'm delivering him to Kilburn myself sometime next week. Pain in the arse."

"Can't say I blame you. I wouldn't want my kid brother, just out of nappies, living with me for a year either," Stanley said, having a laugh at Patrick's expense.

After walking Stanley out to the car park, Patrick beat a path back to his computer and opened the attachment to John's e-mail. Following a quick look at the incident report, the mistake John had mentioned was obvious when he read: "assailant said something unintelligible to the victim before administering a blow to the right side of her head." The probationary constable had logged it in as a mugging, and the DS supervising her had not caught the mistake. But muggers didn't chat with their victims. There was no doubt it was an assault, and he intended to find out who had done it.

Chapter 4

As soon as his shift was over, Patrick drove to see Annie at Queen Mary's Hospital, an ugly box of a building set down in the middle of Putney near Roehampton University. Before going up to her room, he had bought a bouquet of flowers from the hospital gift shop, little changed from the last time he had visited it when he was stationed at Renwick. As a detective constable, he had spent untold hours in the accident and emergency room interviewing victims of car accidents, assault, and domestic violence or taking statements from young people who had gone out on a lash, drinking nearly toxic levels of alcohol. While he waited for the medical staff to finish treating the victim and/or suspect, Patrick passed the time by flirting with the nurses, counting on his reddish-blond hair and blue eyes to draw their attention. The endless hours coppers spent sitting in an A and E waiting room were the reasons why so many of them married nurses, the courtship having begun on the premises.

When he entered the room, Annie was asleep, propped up on pillows, her head swathed in bandages. The right side of her face had taken the brunt of the assault and was bruised and swollen, and she sported a black eye usually reserved for boxers. He knew from the incident report that her assailant had landed a blow to the right side of her head causing nausea and disorientation. When her attacker had released her, she had pitched forward, banging her head, first into wrought-iron fencing, before catching the edge of a low brick wall supporting the railings. The impact had resulted in a mild concussion. In addition to the swelling, the skin on her right cheek had been scraped away, but the abrasions weren't so deep that she would scar. Nothing should mar Annie's flawless complexion, and he remembered the coolness of her cheek resting against his own.

Fortunately, the sound of Patrick moving one of the chairs was enough to awaken the patient and spare him any additional memories. When she saw him, she smiled, causing her to wince from the skin stretching over the cuts on her face that had already begun to heal.

"Patrick, thank you for coming," she said, edging herself up into a sitting position. Her voice was hoarse, but that was to be expected from someone who had had a forearm jammed up against her larynx. "John Stanley rang earlier and told me you might be coming by."

"My pleasure. Well, not actually a pleasure," he said, stumbling, and then handed Annie the flowers to cover up his gaffe. "Sorry about all this."

"Yeah. Wrong place, wrong time," she said, accepting the flowers.

Patrick wasn't the only one who had come bearing gifts. Half the room was filled with stuffed animals and flowers. He didn't get the stuffed-animal bit. For a kid, yeah, but a twenty-six-year-old woman? Annie would end up giving them away to a charity shop.

"So you've had a few visitors," Patrick said, acknowledging the flora and fauna.

"Tons. You just missed the Sisterhood," a core group of six girlfriends, all of whom had grown up with Annie in Chelsea and had stayed in contact despite the tugs and pulls of family and work. "We were laughing so hard, Sister chucked them out as soon as visiting hours ended. So how did *you* get in, Patrick? Your smile or your warrant card? Never mind. I'm pretty sure you didn't need to show your warrant card."

Annie knew Patrick to be an unrepentant flirt, but she also knew that if he was in a relationship, it was all smiles and talk for the ladies, but no action. For Patrick, fidelity was a core principle, and on that matter, he walked the straight and narrow and expected his girlfriend to do the same. No deviation, no excuses.

"What were you doing on Old School Road?" Patrick asked, diving right in.

"I'm taking night courses at Roehampton, and I have a flat near the university. I was walking home."

"When did that happen? The flat, I mean."

"About six months ago. I'm a graduate student in hospital administration, so it made sense to make the move."

"You quit the surgery?"

"Yeah, I got tired of the whole Harley Street plastic surgery scene." Since graduating from university, Annie had worked as a medical assistant at a posh clinic where the rich went to have their noses shaved, faces lifted, tummies tucked, and fat sucked out of their butts. She had never liked the job, but because she needed the experience, she had stuck it out. He was glad to hear she was out of there. "Now, I work at a surgery in Hampden from 8:00 until 2:00. Those hours allow me time to do my coursework and get over to the university."

"Where's your flat?" After giving him the location, Patrick made a face. While a copper at the Renwick nick, there had been an uptick in 999 calls coming into the station from Pullman Crescent, a neighbourhood that had been cut in half when the motorway had been built, basically destroying the cohesiveness of a once prospering middle-class commuter suburb of London. He was less than thrilled with the idea of Annie living there. "You didn't change the address on your driving licence."

"No, officer, I did not. Are you going to arrest me? Did you bring the cuffs?" she said, holding out her hands.

"I didn't mean it like that," Patrick quickly added. "Stanley sent me a copy of the incident report, and it shows your Hammersmith address."

"Like I said, I moved."

Patrick waited for more, and he was good at waiting. When a person came from a large family that included four sisters, you got used to waiting your turn. As a detective, it worked to his advantage. People hated prolonged silences, and the longer it went on, the more likely the person would start talking. Often it was like opening a tap, and the suspect wouldn't shut up.

"It's convenient to my work and flat." Patrick stuck with the silent treatment. "All right, I didn't move to be nearer to uni. Last April, Daphne skipped out and stuck me with the rent. There was no way I could afford the flat on my own."

"Why didn't you get another flat mate?"

Annie rolled her eyes. There were two Patrick Sheas: the handsome man who had swept her off her feet with a smile and a few sentences and the copper—the man who was now asking all these questions.

"Because I didn't want it to happen to me again. So I decided to hell with it. I'd find some place I could afford on my own."

"Sorry. Didn't know about any of that."

"How could you?" Annie said with a shrug of her shoulders. "But what I want to know is: Are you here as a friend or as a copper? Because if you are here in an official capacity, you can get all the details of the attack from DS Shakur, who was the one who interviewed me."

"Except that Detective Sergeant Shakur had you down as being mugged by a bag snatcher. There's no way this was a mugging. You were assaulted."

Although he knew it would unsettle her, Annie had to know that bag snatchers didn't forget to take the handbag or the mobile, and their crimes weren't personal. Whoever had punched Annie in the head had whispered something in her ear. Muggers didn't deliver messages. They grabbed the goods and hauled arse.

"Do you remember what was said to you?"

"No," Annie answered, shaking her head. "He punched me so hard my ears were ringing. I only knew he was talking to me because I could feel his breath on my skin."

"Who would want to do this to you?"

"No one." Patrick stared at her, his eyes boring into her like blue lasers. "Stop looking at me like that." But there was to be no reprieve. "I honestly don't know anyone who would want to do this to me. I do not have enemies. Isn't that the next question? Do you have any enemies? I have to assume it was random or my assailant mistook me for someone else."

"Boyfriend?" Patrick asked, ignoring her comments.

"No."

"Recent breakup?"

"No."

"Breakup within the past year?"

"No, Detective Sergeant Shea," an exasperated Annie answered.

"Listen, Annie, I'm sorry I have to ask you all these questions, but someone pulled you by the hair, punched you in the head, and pushed you into a brick wall. I'm not the bloke you should be pissed off at."

Annie stated once again that she had already answered the same questions with DS Shakur with a follow-up telephone call from Sergeant Stanley of the Renwick nick. "And allow me to reiterate: I don't currently have a boyfriend. In fact, I haven't had a serious relationship since…"

"Since when?"

"…since you and I broke up," she said, shifting uncomfortably in her stiff hospital gown. "Other than a couple of dates with someone months ago, there has been no one."

Patrick found it hard to believe that no man had stepped in to fill the vacancy created by their break-up. Even with her injuries, Annie was beautiful, her Scots ancestors having provided her with a fair complexion that served to enhance her thick black hair and dark eyes.

"What about the bloke you threw me over for?"

"As I mentioned at the time of our break-up, it was a fling, and it lasted only the one night. I have never seen him again," Annie answered while staring at her hands. "Listen, Patrick, I know you are trying to be helpful, but it is the honest-to-God's truth that I haven't been with anyone since we broke up." But then she went quiet for several minutes. "After I decided to leave the clinic, I enrolled at Roehampton to work on a master's degree in hospital administration. It's an intense, one-year programme, and since making that decision, all my efforts have been directed to that end. Once that's behind me, I'll be back in the game. And it's not as if I don't go out. I do have girlfriends. I do go to clubs and put in my time at the neighbourhood pubs, but *I do not have a love interest.*"

"Where are you going after they discharge you?"

"Home. Where else would I go?"

"Your dad's? It would be a good idea to have someone around—at least for a while."

Annie shook her head. "Camille doesn't like me all that much," she said of her father's third wife. "I don't want to upset the apple cart. They've only been married a little more than a year."

"What about your mother?"

"Mum is living in the Highlands."

"Your mother is living in the Scottish Highlands. Why?"

Even before meeting Annie's mother, Patrick had a hint of what Lorna Paget Jameson Parker was like when Annie had described her by singing a few lines from a song from *The Sound of Music*: "How do you find a word that means Maria? A flibbertigibbet, a will-o'-wisp, a clown!" Since her divorce from Mr. Jameson and second husband Nigel Parker, she had flitted about the country and the world following up on articles she had read in travel magazines or *National Geographic*, the money from two divorce settlements providing the wherewithal for her jaunts. Although Annie was guaranteed room and board in her mother's home, Mrs. Jameson Parker kept her cash in her pocket and her credit cards tucked away, staying true to the reputation of the Scots for being a thrifty race.

"Knowing how little you think of my mother as it is, this will only add to it. But because you've asked, I shall tell you."

Annie explained that her mother's parents had grown up in a village west of Aberdeen in a home where Scottish Gaelic was spoken, and her mother had picked up some phrases from her grandmother.

"She's now living in Thurso for the purpose of recording Scottish speakers for posterity. Thurso is about as far north as you can go without getting on a boat and leaving the mainland, so I will not be going home with Mummy."

"Is there a call for what she's doing?"

"Yes, but not from an amateur like my mother. Linguists have been making these recordings for decades—probably since the invention of the radio threatened to anglicise everything. But she feels she has a contribution to make. Truthfully, I prefer her in Thurso rather than a dig in Egypt where she suffered from a serious case of food poisoning that had her in hospital for two weeks."

"If you don't mind me butting into your business," Patrick said, not waiting for a response, "I would rather you not go home until after I have checked out your flat. I want to have a look at the locks, outdoor lighting, places where a villain can hide, etc. Make sure no one can break in."

"Do you think someone would do that?" Annie asked, fear inching into her voice.

"Since there is no way to know why this bloke assaulted you, we really can't say what your assailant is capable of. Better safe than sorry."

"I have mates who can help out."

"Yeah, but I'd feel better if I did it."

Annie reluctantly accepted his offer, but then she never wanted to experience anything like this ever again.

"Now that the interview has concluded, why don't you take off your policeman's hat and just be a friend. I'd love to hear what Josh is doing. I miss him."

Patrick was happy to oblige, and he brought Annie up to date on his son's accomplishments at St. Edmund's and his upcoming holiday to the French Alps. "The little striker misses you as well."

Like his dad, Josh followed Arsenal while Annie was a Chelsea football fan, and the two of them would get into the nitty-gritty details about each of the players and argued about which one had the better team. It was a game they played, and Josh loved it. One of his son's most cherished possessions was an autographed photo from Arsenal midfielder Ray Parlour that Annie had given to him on their only Christmas together.

"We talked about you the last time I had him for a weekend. Josh wanted to know if you were still at the surgery puffing up women's lips and shaving off bits of bone from their noses. He keeps telling me it's gross, but I think that's the attraction and the reason for all the questions."

Annie laughed. "If he thinks that's gross, he should watch a surgeon perform liposuction."

"Don't ever say that to him or he'll call your bluff. You'll be ringing Dr. Tranh so Josh can watch one of his surgeries."

"Yeah, I can easily believe that. He's curious about everything. Just like his dad which is why you're such a good copper."

And why I'm a lousy boyfriend, Patrick thought. But he kept it to himself.

Chapter 5

Patrick arrived at Susan's flat with pizza in hand. After his visit with Annie at the hospital, he had headed home, his mind filled with memories of a relationship that had made him a believer in second chances.

Annie and he had met at an Indian restaurant where they had been sitting at adjacent tables. The flirting between the two had been so obvious that they had lingered after their respective friends had left, and the two of them had stayed in the restaurant until closing. Their first date was a retro night at a suburban cinema celebrating the 60th anniversary of the release of *Casablanca*. By the time Rick Blaine and Captain Renault were walking off into the fog and contemplating the beginning of a beautiful friendship, Patrick knew this was a girl he could fall in love with, and he did.

After leaving Queen Mary's Hospital, his recollections of his time with Annie had him in a funk, and he completely blew Susan off and didn't respond to her three messages—a shitty thing to do.

She really was a nice lady and deserved a decent boyfriend. It just wasn't going to be him. After dinner, he would look for an opening to let her know that she could do better.

"What's this?" Susan asked, staring at the pizza box.

"Last night, I know you rented a DVD..."

"Is there a reason for the no-show?"

"A friend of mine was assaulted near Roehampton University and ended up in hospital."

"Oh, I'm sorry," Susan said, the edge in her voice disappearing. "Why didn't you let me know? I would have understood. How is he doing?"

"*She* is bit of mess actually. Concussion, abrasions, and a black eye. But the docs say she'll be okay."

"Does *she* have a name?"

Patrick made it a hard and fast rule never to discuss previous girlfriends. There was absolutely nothing to be gained in rehashing the reasons why a relationship went south. And he didn't want to hear about old boyfriends either. As a result, Susan knew nothing about Annie, and he knew less than nothing about the men Susan had dated. He wasn't going to change that by telling Susan that Annie was an old flame.

"Her name is Annie. Annie Jameson." Patrick

could tell from Susan's pursed lips that she would have been happier if his hospitalised friend had been male.

"Is that area in your patch?"

"No. I got a courtesy visit from John Stanley, a mate from Renwick, who let me know about the assault. He knew Annie was a friend."

"But Renwick, not Hampden, will actually handle the case. Yes?" she asked, the edge back in her voice.

"Yes. They'll take good care of her." Hoping it would put an end to the questions, he went into the kitchen and got the plates out for the pizza.

During dinner, little was said. Although he had never mentioned Annie, for some reason, Patrick felt as if Susan knew that Annie Jameson was more than just a friend—a lot more than a friend. In fact, Annie and he had talked about getting married and having a kid.

The problem was, if Susan *did* know about Annie and he broke up with her tonight, she would think it was because of Annie, and it had absolutely nothing to do with her. Or was he kidding himself? Was it possible he had never got over Annie? With that thought, a weariness overtook him, and he slumped in his chair. Susan, sensing the change in his mood, leant over and kissed him.

"I still have the DVD, and we can watch it in bed."

Bone weary and mentally exhausted, Patrick nodded and pushed away from the table.

* * *

With Susan still asleep, Patrick had hoped to slip out of the flat without waking her. But he had only got his trousers on when she chirped a good morning and offered to make him a hot breakfast, an offer he declined because he just wanted to get out of there. Seeing her blonde hair cascading over her breasts only served to depress him. If he had a backbone, before going to bed, he would have told her it was never going to work. Instead, they had had sex. Mentally, he felt like a louse, but physically he was feeling pretty good.

One reason why their relationship wasn't going to work was because Susan and he were seriously mismatched, the attraction being entirely physical, at least on his part. Although Susan spent a fortune on fashion and celebrity magazines, she never read a book nor did she follow politics or current events. If she picked up a newspaper, it was a tabloid. She seemed content to remain completely ignorant of the epic events taking place in the world. Even though her life—everyone's life—had changed with the attacks in New York and Washington by radical Islamists two years earlier, as far as she was concerned, it had nothing to do with her because if it did, her clients at Sun Kissed would be talking about it. Because all her friends were members of the tanning salon, her workplace formed the nucleus of her world. She loved her job, exercised with her mates at a neighbourhood health club, lived near her favourite fish and chip shop, and had a good-looking boyfriend who was gainfully employed. For Susan, everything was coming up roses. This narrow worldview worked for her, but it made Patrick claustrophobic.

"Sorry to wake you," Patrick said while slipping into his shoes.

"No problem," she answered, scooting across the bed and wrapping her arms around him. "I like it better when I get to say goodbye to you. I'm never sure when I'll see my man again."

"True enough," he said, patting her hand. "I'll tell you now that I won't be over for the next few days. Jack and I are cleaning my flat. He moves out exactly one week tomorrow, and I want him to mop up his own shit before he goes. If I don't watch him, he'll sit on his arse all day working the remote" *and screwing Robin, his co-worker from the video store, in his big brother's bed.*

"I can help with that."

"You wouldn't say that if you saw my flat," he answered, shaking his head at the memory of a sink full of dishes and dirty clothes everywhere but in the laundry basket. "I would have never believed my brother was capable of living in a pig sty. If my mum saw my flat, she would have his hide."

"Many hands make light work. That's what my mother always said," Susan answered, repeating her offer.

"Mine as well, but you are *not* my cleaner," he said emphatically ruling out any further offers of help. "After that, I'll be at the station trying to finish up the paperwork on the Hampden Burglar. The last robbery made a total of six, so there's a fair amount of paperwork to get in order, plus I have to get started on an effectiveness report for DC Updike. Her six-month review is coming up."

"Well, let me know if you change your mind. I'll bring my own mop."

Chapter 6

Patrick smiled at a gap-toothed teen, the eldest of three children of Sergeant John Stanley. Jenna was about fifteen-years-old, old enough to flirt with a co-worker of her father's, even if he was fourteen years her senior. Because he was left-handed, they had been rubbing elbows throughout dinner, and Patrick could tell that Jenna was enjoying the contact. Discreet smiles from her parents let him know that they found the exchange amusing.

The Stanleys were a downsized version of Patrick's own family of eight, and just like the Shea clan at mealtime, there was the loud hum of conversation with each sibling trying to talk over the other in an effort to gain their parents' attention. *Good luck with that*, Patrick thought, while thinking of an average night at the Shea dinner table.

After helping to clear the dishes, John and Patrick went into a little cubbyhole that served as a home office and where John kept the scotch in a locked liquor cupboard.

"You were right, John. I did go to see Annie,"

Patrick said after accepting the offered drink. He explained that Annie had tried to convince him that the assault was either a random attack or a case of mistaken identity, but Patrick wasn't buying it.

"It *could* be a case of mistaken identity," John said. "When I found out it was Annie who was attacked, I drove out to the scene and had a look myself. That street is dark with all trees covering up the lampposts, and the houses are set back so far that you don't get any light from them either. Because that particular section of Old School Road dead ends into the heath, with a footpath used by the students attending Roehampton, Annie's assailant could have been waiting for anyone who used it as a shortcut to High Street."

"But what was she doing on that street anyway?"

Like John, after learning of Annie's assault, he had retraced her route, but it had left him with more questions than answers. If Annie was going from the library to her flat, she had walked past two bus stops. The only reason he could think of for her doing that was she was trying to save money on a bus transfer. If that were the case, then something was definitely out of whack. Annie's father was a portfolio manager for an investment firm with some big-name clients. Although Patrick didn't particularly care for Mr. Jameson, for the most part, he had done okay by Annie: helping her with rent and living expenses. Or had that changed with the slowdown resulting from the terrorist attacks in America or possibly his marriage to the third Mrs. Jameson had proved to be more expensive than he had anticipated?

"When I asked Annie about it, she dodged the question, telling me that she liked to walk," Stanley said, interrupting Patrick's musings. "I cautioned her that it was not a good idea to be out there on her own, especially at that time of night and most especially on the heath. You and I know it's a favourite place for druggies. Regardless of why she was there, this was no run-of-the-mill bag snatcher. If it were a snatch, he's a major cock-up or he's just starting out in a life of crime. A pro would not forget to take the handbag," Stanley said. "Another thing. You don't punch someone in the head and *then* whisper in their ear, thinking they're gonna hear you with all them bells ringing. And what the hell would a mugger say? 'Thank you for your donation to a worthy cause?'"

Stanley's statement bolstered Patrick's theory that Annie was the target. "Annie told DS Shakur that there was someone walking down the street on the opposite side. I think he may have been her assailant. After checking to make sure she was his target, he doubled back."

"That's certainly possible."

"Does the dog walker's story check out?" Patrick asked.

"Yeah. He's an assistant professor at

Roehampton. University records show he never had Annie as a student. Because his dog's old and has bladder problems, he's out a couple of times a night with the mutt because he's not ready to put her down. He had more to say about the dog than the assault. What are you thinking? An old boyfriend?"

"Annie says there's been no one since we called it quits. But come on, John! You've seen her. How can someone so beautiful not have a man in her life for the last fifteen months?"

"Well, this may come as a surprise to you, Patrick, but not every woman *wants* a man in her life, especially if her last relationship had a rough landing."

Patrick agreed that that was certainly a possibility. Unlike a lot of women, Annie didn't think it was necessary to be on the arm of a man in order to be fulfilled. There was also the bitter aftertaste left by her parents' divorce and remarriages and another reason why they had never moved in together. There had already been too many packed boxes and goodbyes in Annie's life.

"It's funny that all of this is happening now," Patrick continued. "I didn't see Annie for more than a year, and now I've seen her three times in the last month."

Patrick explained that he had run into Annie when he had been withdrawing some money from a cashpoint machine near his flat in Renwick. When he had turned around, she was behind him in line, and the shock of seeing her for the first time since their split had left him speechless. She asked about his family and Josh; he asked about her parents and the job. That was it. He hadn't been that awkward with a girl since secondary school.

The next meeting at Tesco's went smoother. One of the things Patrick liked best about Annie was her voice. The first thing he did after finishing a shift was to ring Annie. Talking to her was a stress reliever, allowing him to jettison some of the more stressful events of the day—at least for a while. If they couldn't get together for the night, they would just talk. After being denied hearing her husky alto for a year, the sound of her voice had been like a balm on an old wound.

"Listen, Patrick, I'm really sorry this happened to Annie," Stanley said, pulling Patrick's head out of the clouds, "but looking at it from a copper's point of view, I've got nothing to go on. We put notices up all over the place, including nearby sandwich and chip shops, pubs, students' union, bus stops, etc. Didn't get so much as a nibble, which is what I expected. If there were any witnesses, it would likely have been someone from the university, and how many students do you know who would want to spend an afternoon at a police station being interviewed? For most people, violence is what happens to someone else. No one thinks it's their responsibility to help solve a crime until it happens to them."

"I don't like the idea of someone targeting Annie."

"Understandable. And if *you* want to run with this, that's fine with me, but there's no way Superintendent Lawrence will agree to put any manpower on it—not with what we've got right now. You probably already know that someone tried to start a fire in the skip outside the mosque on Davis Street, and the walls were tagged with racial epitaphs. That one ended up on the telly. And we've had two armed assaults this week alone. Hate crimes and crimes involving weapons are getting all the attention and manpower."

There was another reason no one at the Renwick nick would be put on the Jameson assault. With increasing pressure from the Metropolitan Police to bolster the "clear rate," there were few superintendents who would agree to an enquiry of a crime with no witnesses or motive. It messed with the statistics.

"Why don't you talk to your governor? There's some overlap between Renwick and Hampden," Stanley suggested. "Craig might let you spend some time on it. Mention to him that Annie's a friend and see what happens."

Patrick laughed. There was no way his super

would allow any of his officers to investigate an assault that had happened on someone else's patch. Everything with Craig was by the book.

"But if you do decide to go off radar, keep your head down and my name out of it," Stanley added. "But if you find anything, let me know, and I'll see what I can do. But it's not going to be easy. Honestly, I don't even know where to tell you to start."

"I think I'll start with Annie's former flat mate, Daphne Pierson. She might know if Annie attracted the attention of some nutter. These days, it doesn't take much."

"Too right," Stanley said, nodding his head in agreement. "Just remember, if your guv rings, I don't know anything."

Chapter 7

"We've got a crier for you in Interview Room 2," the front desk sergeant said shortly after Patrick pushed through the door of the Hampden police station. "Kid went missing."

As soon as Patrick heard "kid," the muscles in his stomach tightened. His first murder, and the worst crime scene he had ever worked, had been the death of a little girl at the hands of her mother's boyfriend. He had been a uniformed cop assigned to logging in everyone who entered the house where the five-year-old had been murdered, and he had seen detectives with years of experience with tear-stained faces. There was no amount of training or experience that could prepare you for the death of a child.

"How old?"

"Seventeen," he said, handing Patrick a box of tissues.

"Is DC Updike in yet?" he asked relieved that the kid was a teenager. It was more likely that a seventeen-year-old girl would have run away with a boyfriend rather than being abducted.

"Yeah, she's getting Mrs. Ryff some coffee."

"I'd like a cup myself. It's bloody freezing out there."

As soon as Patrick entered the room, he recognised Mrs. Ryff. Although he had not been the one to interview her, he knew her from an earlier visit to the station when her daughter had gone missing at least one other time. This was good. If the kid had run off before, it was likely she had done it again. After introducing himself, Patrick explained that it would be necessary to wait for DC Updike to return so that there would be another officer present for the interview.

"I don't care about that," Mrs. Ryff said while tossing another tissue into a bin approaching the tipping point. "I want my Tanya back." But Patrick leaned back in his chair to show the woman that rules were rules.

After Molly arrived with three coffees in a carrier, Patrick began the interview, and it appeared that this was the usual story of a teen running off after a bust-up at home. The only difference this time was that it had happened four days earlier.

"Why did you wait so long to report Tanya as missing?" Patrick asked.

"Last time I was here, your lot told me to wait a day or two to see if she turned up."

"And did she?"

"Yeah, but tonight will be the fifth night she's been gone. I think something's happened to her," she said, dabbing at her eyes. After balling up the tissues, she added it to the pile.

"Is there any evidence to indicate she was taken against her will?"

"No," Mrs. Ryff answered. "But she's been running with a rough crowd."

"By 'a rough crowd,' do you mean drugs?"

"I don't know. What I do know is that the loser she's been seeing was on the inside for nicking cars."

"What's the lad's name?"

"Denny Fisher." Patrick noted the name in his notebook. "He used to live on Logan Lane, but his sister chucked him out."

"Does Tanya have a mobile?"

Mrs. Ryff shook her head. "That's what the row was about. The telephone bill came in the post, and Tanya went way over on her minutes. Last month when it was £15 over, my husband tore into her and told her he'd take her phone away if ever she went over again, and this month it was even higher. When Alan saw that, he went through the rafters. Tanya had the mobile in her hand, and when Alan tried to grab it, it went flying against the wall. It's in pieces back at the house."

"It would be helpful if you could bring the mobile

into the station. In that way, we can have our technicians access her contact list. Her friends might know where she's been spending the night."

"Good luck with that," Mrs. Ryff said, snorting. "I've called all her friends, and no one knows nothing."

"That might change if the call came from a police station."

At that point, Molly cleared her throat, an indication that she had questions of her own. Noting that the mother's name was different from her daughter's, she asked if Mr. Ryff was Tanya's stepdad. Patrick looked at his partner and nodded in approval. It was his experience that a stepdad often complicated the picture.

"Yeah, but we've been married for five years. Five years! And she still tells me she's not used to having anyone but her dad in the house. Blimey, she hasn't seen her dad in a year! I know Tanya doesn't like Alan, but what she's got to understand is that he's the one who pays the bills. If it weren't for Alan, she wouldn't even have a mobile."

"Did the row get physical?" Molly asked.

"Not really. When Alan grabbed the phone out of her hand, Tanya tried to grab it back. When she pulled away from him, she fell backwards. But she wasn't hurt. I know she wasn't. But it would be just like her to say otherwise—if you know what I mean.

She's a drama queen."

Patrick did know what she meant. The dynamics in a blended family were complicated and often volatile, and he counted his blessings that Ally had found a prince among men when she had married the boring Dr. Peter Petrie, but that worked to Patrick's advantage. No matter where he took his son, it would seem interesting compared to the outings Josh had with his stepdad, a man big on visiting museums and historic sites. Patrick understood that a trip to the Victoria and Albert Museum was not at the top of an eight-year-old's must-see list.

"I see you have provided DC Updike with a list of your daughter's friends," he said, glancing at the lined paper on the table with numbers next to each name. Molly had suggested that Mrs. Ryff prioritise the list of those most likely to know of Tanya's whereabouts. "We'll need to know where her friends hang out."

"You'll want to start by looking for the boyfriend down at the arcade. I told Tanya to stay away from that Fisher boy because he's no good. But she kept on seeing him. Doesn't give a brass farthing about what I think."

"Is Fisher violent?"

"I don't think so, but like I said, he was inside for nicking cars."

The fact that her daughter was seeing someone with a prison record was obviously Mrs. Ryff's biggest fear. Would Fisher do something illegal that would end up with her daughter serving time as well?

After Mrs. Ryff had shared everything she knew, the interview was concluded, and Molly and Patrick checked the computer to see what else they had on Fisher. Although he had an extensive juvenile record, mostly for shoplifting and minor vandalism, there was nothing in his file to indicate he was violent. His record as an adult showed a few run-ins with the cops and arrests for breaches of peace, but no convictions until he had been caught stealing a Mercedes from a car park. The vehicle had been recovered the next day.

"He's obviously not the brightest bulb in the pack," Molly said, scanning the computer screen and the report on the car theft.

"Yeah," Patrick agreed. "He didn't think anyone would notice a red 2002 Mercedes parked on a street in a rundown section of Hampden. But I like it when they're this stupid. It's so easy to find them."

While putting on his coat, Patrick told Molly to start telephoning the friends on Mrs. Ryff's list and to follow up with the mother in emphasising the importance of getting the mobile to the station. "Also ring Fisher's probation officer to see if he has an address for him. I'm going to start with the arcade."

"You going alone?" Molly asked. "You pushing off on me, DS Shea?"

"I'm actually doing you a good turn. You won't have to go outside in this freezing weather." Molly made a face indicating she wasn't buying it. "Okay. There is another reason. I need a favour." He shared with his partner the attack on Annie Jameson. It was the personal element of the assault that continued to worry him, and he asked Molly to get Annie's telephone records.

"Any reason why Renwick isn't doing this?"

"Low priority. Actually, according to Sergeant John Stanley of the Renwick nick, no priority."

"Because...?"

"Because they haven't got so much as a whiff of a lead and they are working two assaults involving weapons and a hate crime. Stanley told me that if I got him something with some meat on it that that might change, but in the meantime, I'm it."

"If someone asks what I'm working on, what do I say?"

"Tell the truth. You're working on the Ryff case." Patrick flashed Molly the smile that got him pretty much everything he wanted—at least from the female constables.

Chapter 8

The arcade was a dying institution. With most kids having access to a home computer and video games available at the local video store, they didn't need to venture out beyond their own front door to play the games. It was only those with few friends or losers with plenty of friends, but the wrong kind, who continued to find the noise and lights of video games alluring.

As Patrick entered the arcade, the smell of burnt popcorn permeated everything, and there was enough of it on the floor to supply a cinema. The "manager" was a twenty-year-old kid whose job was to sell tokens and to make sure no one damaged the machines. But with his eyes focused on the breasts of a centrefold in a porn magazine, he wasn't even doing that. If someone backed a truck up to the back door and emptied the place, Patrick doubted he would even bother to ring the police.

After Patrick showed the manager his warrant card, the kid said there was nothing he could do about kids who wanted to smoke weed. "I ain't a copper."

"I'm not here about cannabis, Garick," he said, reading the name off the name tag. "I'm looking for this young lady. Her name's Tanya Dorsett, and she hangs out with Denny Fisher. Does the name ring a bell?"

"I ain't seen Denny in a while, but Lem, his errand boy, comes in now and then. He's living in a squat on the South Hill estate."

"Do you know where on the estate?" Patrick asked referring to a crumbling high-rise complex built in the late sixties. It was slated for demolition, that is, as soon as people stopped arguing about what entity would pay for it.

"Dunno."

"Do you know anyone who does?" After struggling to lift his finger to point to a tough working a joy stick, Patrick asked if he had a name.

"Danny Hunter."

"Oh, it's Danny Hunter, is it? He's in here when he's not acting in *Spooks*. Is that right?" Patrick asked, referring to the popular television series.

"Dunno," Garrick said, laughing.

After leaving his card, Patrick went over to talk to Danny Hunter and showed him a picture of Tanya. After puzzling over the photo, the kid let out a puff of smoke in the direction of Patrick's face. But Patrick refused to bite. No sense giving the little shit a bigger ego by over-reacting.

"If you skip the lecture about how bad smoking is for me," the kid began, "I'll tell you that Lem is in 4B."

"You are overestimating my concern for your health," Patrick said in his best "I don't give a shit" voice. "Do you know if this girl is with him?"

"Dunno."

"Dunno or won't say?"

"What's in it for me?"

"The gratitude of a nation," Patrick said, walking away, convinced he didn't know anything else.

After telephoning the station to ask that a panda car meet him at the South Hill estate, Patrick decided to walk. He wanted to get the stale smells of the arcade out of his nostrils. There was another reason. If he parked the car on estate property, he risked slashed tires, a broken windscreen, or, possibly, his car going missing. But after ten minutes and with frigid air pouring into his lungs, he wondered if saving a seven-year-old police car was really all that important.

While waiting for the panda car, he thought about what he would encounter once he entered the complex. The stairwells would be filled with discarded drug paraphernalia and the smells of urine and excrement from broken, but still used, toilets. Fleeting shadows would spread the news that a copper was in the building, and his every step would be watched by eyes peering out at him through torn curtains. Behind the numbered doors were people who had plummeted to the bottom of society because, if they hadn't, they would no longer be calling South Hill home.

After flagging down the police car, Patrick motioned to the officers that he wanted to get in the back seat, and he heard the lock click open. Owen Llewellyn and Greg Grant had been partners for a decade. There wasn't anything the two hadn't seen or done, including getting shot at during a bank robbery gone wrong, and they knew their patch better than their own back gardens.

"Good morning, gents. Lovely weather we're having," Patrick began.

"Shea, you must be a nutter walking around in this weather. I can't even take a piss for fear my dick will freeze up and fall off," Llewellyn answered.

"Now, the missus wouldn't want that *or* would she?"

"She takes all I'm willing to give her," Llewellyn answered, grabbing his balls.

"Enough with the macho shit," Grant said. "What have you got for us, Paddy?"

"Seventeen-year-old Tanya Dorsett went missing following a row with her stepdad," he said, handing Grant a photo of the missing teen. "She's done it once before, but the last time she was gone only two days.

Today is the fifth day, and her mum's worried sick. She thinks she's hiding out with her boyfriend, Denny Fisher. The little shit of a manager at the arcade said I needed to talk to a bloke named Lem, Denny Fisher's errand boy, and that I could find him on the estate."

"Lem is Lee Mason, a lad with his IQ written in red ink, but he wouldn't hurt a fly," Grant said. "Although he's only nineteen, he's been living rough or holing up in one of the squats for a couple of years now. Denny offers him some protection from the gangs on the estate. In return, he does whatever Denny asks him to, but it's usually nothing illegal as the kid's a mental midget and would screw it up for sure.

"As for Denny Fisher, he got out of prison for nicking cars about a month ago. Since then, he's been selling enough cannabis to keep him in groceries. At the moment, he's flying under radar, and we've had no reason to try to find out where he's living because we don't get overly excited about marijuana, not with the amount of cocaine and meth sold on the estate. Knowing Denny, I can tell you there's no way he would hole up in a squat in South Hill. He's a pretty boy and has standards, especially if he's trying to impress Miss Dorsett. She's a good looking kid."

Patrick showed the officers the address Molly had got from Fisher's probation officer; both shook their heads. "That's Fisher's sister's address," Grant said, "but I know Denny's not there because yesterday we hauled her son's arse into the nick for vandalism. While arresting her kid, we asked her about her brother, but she said Denny knew better than to show up at her house. She said she'd kick his arse all the way to Brighton if ever he did."

"She's got a one-criminal quota for living in her house," Llewellyn said, chuckling.

"What about Lem? Is he around?"

"He should be in," Llewellyn answered. "You want to play good cop/bad cop?"

"Which one am I?" Patrick asked.

"You've got to be kidding? With your baby face, who'd ever take you for a villain? Besides, as soon as Lem sees me, he'll shit his pants." The six-foot-three Welshman got out of the car and put on his game face.

As they made their way to 4B, Llewellyn said nothing, probably because words required deeper breaths, and the cold air made breathing painful. The door was answered by the man himself wearing a torn and faded Arsenal hoodie, a scraggly underfed lad in his late teens with a serious case of acne. After inviting themselves in, the Welshman checked the other rooms to make sure Lem was alone and that there would be no surprises. The flat was surprisingly neat. Blankets of all shapes and sizes, probably picked up from a charity shop, were neatly folded and piled up in a corner, a sure tip-off that a female had recently been in residence.

"Do you know the whereabouts of this young lady," Patrick asked, showing Lem Tanya's photo.

"I've seen her around."

"Would *around* include this flat?"

"She's Denny Fisher's bird. I dunno nuffin'."

"Do you know the girl is only seventeen?" Llewelyn asked while inching closer to Lem. "That creates all kinds of problems for you, you being an adult and all."

"Yeah! Well, seventeen ain't fifteen," Lem answered, trying to stand his ground.

"Not good enough," Patrick said. "According to Section 47 of the just passed Sexual Offences Act, Denny, who is over eighteen, is in a position of trust with regard to Miss Dorset, and as such, it is illegal for Denny to engage in any sexual activity with the girl."

"But she ain't *my* bird, and I dunno where she is."

"You the one tidying up in here?" Llewellyn asked, pointing to the folded blankets.

"Tanya come 'round crying that her stepdad kicked her out of the house, and she needed a place to stay. But that was days ago."

"What happened days ago?"

"Denny come and fetched her. I swear to God that's all I know."

"Really?" Llewellyn asked, practically breathing Lem's air. "I'm not so sure about that. I think a trip to the nick might refresh your memory. Give us a chance to check to see if you've got form since the last time we chatted."

"You know I was in juvie for joyriding, but I ain't done nuffin' wrong since. I swear." Even though the room was unheated and the cops could see their breath, the kid was sweating.

"Well, we're going to check it out anyway. You might want to put on a coat—if you got one. It's colder than a witch's teat out there."

Now that Llewellyn had set the stage, it was time for Patrick to play his part as Lem's saviour. "Officer Llewellyn, wait a minute," Patrick said, stepping between the two. "Maybe Lem doesn't fully understand the situation." He turned his back to Llewellyn and faced Lem. "What I think we've got here is a girl—Tanya—who's pissed off at her parents, and she's trying to punish them by not coming home. But I can't be sure about that, now can I? So if I don't find Tanya, say, within the next twenty-four hours, I'm going to have to look differently at her going missing. Instead of a runaway, I might think she was taken against her will." Lem's eyes shifted to the uniformed officer to see if DS Shea was having him on, and Llewellyn's grim look was his answer. "At the very least, we might be looking at corrupting a minor or, at worst, kidnapping."

"You're shitting me, man. She come looking for Denny—not the other way 'round."

"So *you* say, but like *I* said, I've got to be sure," Patrick continued. "So here's the deal. You find out where Denny and Tanya are staying and pay them a visit. While you're talking to Tanya, you might mention that she'll be eighteen in five months. All she has to do is suck it up for that short amount of time. Then she can do whatever she wants because she'll be an adult. Now, you look like an intelligent fellow," Patrick said, lying, "so I'm sure you can see the wisdom of this particular approach to the problem." Lem nodded. "I want to be clear about this. Tanya needs to ring her parents as soon as possible just to let them know she's all right. Twenty-four hours. That's all I'm giving you to find Fisher. After that, we'll be breaking down doors looking for the girl, and you might end up going down as an accessory. Are we on the same page?" Lem again nodded. "Thank you for your help."

"I'll give him five minutes, and he'll be out of that flat heading straight for Fisher," Llewellyn said as soon as the door to the flat closed behind them. "I didn't think it was possible for that pasty prat to get any paler, but our little talk sucked the colour right out of his face. He looked like a vampire's lunch."

Patrick hoped Llewellyn was right about Lem leading them to Fisher. It didn't happen often, but sometimes all it took was a visit from a copper to get results, and the Welshman was famous for getting results. Llewellyn radioed his partner to let him know he would be tailing Lem as soon as he set foot outside the flat.

"Don't know if we can stay with him, Paddy, but if he shakes us, I've a pretty good idea where's he headed."

Llewellyn's estimate for Lem's emergence from the flat was off by two minutes; he was out in three. The teenager disappeared over a four-foot concrete wall, and there was no way they could follow an agile youth running at full speed, so the pair of coppers headed back to the car.

"He's probably headed for Jimmy McGrath's house, Denny's best mate," Grant said when Llewellyn told him about their chat with Lem. "We'll head over there now and let you know if we find the girl."

After getting a ride to his car, Patrick headed back to the station. He had no idea how this would play out. Lem could do a runner, and he'd have to start over. But he was feeling reasonably confident that his argument, and the threat of a second visit from Llewellyn, would be persuasive—at least he hoped so. He had no wish to go back to the misery that was South Hill.

* * *

"Blimey, Patrick, what did you say and who did you

say it to?" Molly asked as soon as Patrick got back to the station. "Tanya Dorsett rang her mother a half hour ago."

Having received a report from Officer Grant en route to the station, Patrick already knew the girl had been found and that the policemen were in the process of personally delivering the Dorsett girl to her mother. After explaining his part in the good cop/bad cop routine with Lem, Molly started laughing. "You scared the shit out of the kid. That's what you did." She shook her head in amazement. Patrick had the face of an altar boy, one that wouldn't instil fear in a toddler, no less someone living in a squat. But there was something in his voice and the way he modulated his tone that got people's attention. And here was the proof.

"All it takes is for someone to touch the hem of my gown, and their lives change," he said, sitting on the corner of her desk. "Are you going to write me up for a commendation?"

"Your Irish charm is wasted on me, Shea. I only have eyes for my Eddie and Colin Firth. But, seriously, it will be a relief for Mrs. Ryff to have her daughter home. She told me that when Tanya rang her, she was crying her eyes out. It seems life on the run wasn't all it was cracked up to be."

"Honestly, it had more to do with Llewellyn and Grant than me. They had a good idea where Lem was headed after he left the estate, and they were five minutes behind him. According to Llewellyn, by the time they got to the house where Fisher and Tanya were holed up, Fisher had taken off, but Tanya was still there like a little mouse caught in a trap. So it looks like it's case closed. I don't know what it is, but lately things have been going my way. Mind you, I'm not complaining."

After looking around to see if anyone was eavesdropping, an occupational hazard of working in close quarters with people who were paid to be nosy, Patrick asked his partner if she had been able to get started on filing a request for Annie's phone records. But contacting the telephone company hadn't been necessary because the Renwick station still had Annie's mobile in its evidence locker, and it was merely a matter of going through her call list, something the Renwick police had already done. Like a lot of people, Annie rarely deleted anything, and it was all there at the touch of a thumb.

"Who's on the phone list?"

Molly pretended to stifle a yawn. "I can inform you that your ex-girlfriend leads a boring life. According to DS Shakur, Annie phones her mum who lives somewhere in Scotland, her dad in Chelsea, and some friends here in town. She has her academic advisor on speed dial..."

"What's his name?" Patrick asked, his interest

piqued.

"*Her* name is Mrs. Burton, and Shakur said she sounded ancient. And that's about it, except..."

"Except what?"

"Except that in the last two months, Annie has received an unusual number of phone calls, eight at last count, made from a pay-as-you-go phone that last about a minute. It was bought from a mini market in Renwick, but that's all Shakur was able to find out."

"The phone calls lasted a minute? That's a long time for a hang-up, but long enough to try to figure out if Annie's at home."

"That's my take on it as well. Another thing— there haven't been any calls from that phone since the attack. Maybe this is a case of a love affair gone wrong or a rejected suitor."

With Annie being so insistent that there was no man in her life, Patrick had to take her word that she hadn't had a serious relationship since their breakup. However, there was the possibility that she was being stalked by someone from the university.

Molly agreed that stalking was a possible scenario. "You'll need to talk to her to find out if she gave anyone the brush-off at Roehampton."

"Once she gets out of the hospital, I'm supposed to go with her to her flat to check it out. It'll give me another chance to talk to her about what happened on Old School Road and mention our theory about a

72

stalker."

"It sounds like a plan. But keep in mind the university has an enrolment of 9,000 students or at least that's what their website says."

"Yeah. But right now it's all I got."

Chapter 9

Surveying the street, Patrick couldn't think of one reason why Daphne Pierson had abandoned Annie's flat in Hammersmith to move into an unkempt rowhouse in a decaying section of North London. The tiny garden fronting the three-story building was overrun with weeds poking through a chain-link fence with advert flyers and soft-drink cups forming a type of edging. The one attempt to brighten up the place was a cracked flowerpot sporting an unrecognisable skeleton of a plant that had given up the ghost ages ago. After leaning on the doorbell and knocking on the door several times, Patrick walked back to the sidewalk to see if there was any indication that anyone was moving around inside. None.

"If you're looking for Daphne, she's not home. Just saw her at the market," an older woman called out and pointed to her shopping bags as evidence. "She'll be along in a tick."

"Ta," Patrick called out to the moving figure and returned to his car and its heater to wait for Daphne. Although unhappy that she had stiffed Annie for the rent, he wasn't surprised. Daphne had two part-time jobs, one as a dog groomer in a pet shop and a second as a dog walker. Both were hit and miss, and with a soft economy, he was sure it was mostly miss. On the other hand, it was difficult for him to believe Annie had relied on Daphne's wages to help pay the rent. That would be the equivalent of counting on winning the lottery to pay your bills.

Fifteen minutes later, Annie's former flat mate came into view swinging a plastic grocery bag. There was no doubt the figure walking toward him was Daphne Pierson. Patrick recognised the long angular face framed by spiked bleached-blonde hair. With her leather jacket, oversized glasses, and flowing scarf, she looked like a World War I aviator.

Other than a shared affection for dogs of any breed, Annie and Daphne had nothing in common. He wasn't even sure how their friendship had got its start. All he really knew about her was that she would often crash at Annie's flat when she and her boyfriend had a row—which averaged out to be about twice a week. He never got used to waking up at Annie's and finding Daphne sprawled out on the couch wearing a tee shirt and thong underwear with her skinny butt and "puppy power" tattoo in full view.

"Hello, Daphne," Patrick said as the young women fumbled in her oversized bag for her keys.

"Jesus, Patrick! You scared the shit out of me. What the hell are you doing here?"

"I need to ask you some questions," a statement

that caused Daphne to blanch. "May I come in?" He didn't wait for an answer and stepped into the entryway.

"Give me a minute to straighten up, will ya?" she said while opening the door to her flat.

"If you've got a back door and you go out it, I'll be upset with you," he said and encouraged her to leave the door ajar. After recognising the smell of an air deodoriser, he knew the flat would reek of weed. "I'm not with Narcotics," he shouted into the void. "I want to talk to you about Annie Jameson."

"What about Annie?" Daphne said, appearing out of the mist.

"I'll tell you over a cup of tea."

While inhaling the steam from the hot brew, Patrick summarised Annie's assault and waited for Daphne's response. Instead, she stared into her tea, and he could tell she was crying. With tears streaming down her face, she told Patrick it was all her fault; if she hadn't moved in with Raymond, Annie would never have been attacked.

"You moved out months ago. I don't think you can be held responsible for an attack that happened five days ago. Now, the rent's another matter." Patrick's jab hit its mark.

"Annie will be happy to hear that Raymond did the same thing to me what I did to Annie. Took off and left me with the rent. I am now sharing this flat with a cow I can't stand."

"I don't think that would make Annie happy," Patrick said, explaining that her former flatmate had had to move because she couldn't get by without Daphne's half of the rent.

"Half! That's a laugh. I never paid half—not once," she said as if she were proud that she had been unable to pay her full share. "Annie never depended on me for the rent. The reason money is so tight is because her dad quit sending her money on account of the newest Mrs. Jameson didn't like the idea of her husband passing his kid a few quid and put a stop to it. Her dad's got a boat what he keeps down at Eastbourne and owning a boat is expensive or that's what Mr. Jameson told Annie."

This explanation made a lot more sense than Annie relying on an underemployed halfwit to pay the rent. He also knew Annie adored her father and would be loathe to say anything negative about him. Considering that Mr. Jameson had cheated on his first wife with Annie's mother and had cheated on Lorna with his third wife, he never understood why Annie held him in such high regard. Although the man made buckets of money and gave his only child an allowance, he always took care of himself first: flashy cars, a pied-a-terre in London, a country house in Surrey, and now a boat. It was only because Annie's mother had secured a generous, and watertight, pre-nuptial agreement that she had emerged from their divorce smelling like a rose. It appeared that the big loser in the divorce was Annie.

"But I don't get what I have to do with Annie's attack," Daphne said.

"The assault was premeditated."

"Pre-medicated?"

"Premeditated," Patrick repeated. "That means the attack was planned." He knew Daphne had left school at sixteen to go to work, but even allowing for an abbreviated education, Daphne's gauges all pointed to "empty."

"After punching her in the head, Annie's assailant whispered something in her ear, and that makes it personal," Patrick elaborated. This remark was followed by a "nobody's home" look. "In other words, she knew her attacker. Usually these types of assaults end up tied to a former love interest."

"Do you mean a boyfriend?" Patrick nodded. Daphne's response was to shake her head and to keep shaking it. "No love interest while I was living with her."

"Annie mentioned she had gone out with the same man two or three times. Do you know anything about him?"

"Oh yeah. The ponce from Kensington. She met him at the surgery when he came to pick up his mum after she had Botox injections," Daphne said, puffing out her lips, but then resumed shaking her head, but with even greater emphasis. "You know how couples have body language. Well, Annie and that bloke had zero. He was interested in *her*, but Annie wasn't interested in *him*. It was real obvious. The one time I met him was the only time he come 'round the flat. Let's just say the two of them never had a sleepover, if you take my meaning."

"Do you remember his name?" Patrick asked, pleased to hear that Annie had not been intimate with anyone since their breakup. But after fifteen months, why did he even care?

"Yeah, I remember his name: Terrence Berry. I remember it because he would have been Terry Berry. When he told me what it was, I had a fit of the giggles."

After that statement, Patrick asked Daphne to remind him of how Annie and she had met because Daphne made Susan look like a complex personality.

"We met on account of Mr. Pip. Whenever Annie's mum went abroad, she would ask Annie to watch her Yorkie, and we'd meet up in the park."

From that point on, it was a trip down memory lane with Mr. Pip in the starring role. Patrick disliked most lap dogs, barking bundles of fur, but he *hated* Mr. Pip. When the dog wasn't yapping, he was begging for food or scratching at the door to get out or trying to sleep between Annie and him in bed. When he was growing up, the Shea family had had a

Rottweiler. Now *that* was a dog.

"What about the fellow she threw me over for? Do you know his name?" Patrick asked, steering the conversation away from the Yorkie.

"Oh, the mystery man? Never met him. After you dumped her, Annie was pretty upset. Cried all the time. When I asked her about it, she said it was a one-night stand, and she would pay for her mistake for the rest of her life."

With cops being notorious for getting some on the side, Annie and Patrick had discussed cheating at length. Both understood the consequences of being unfaithful. But was Daphne right? Did Annie consider her one-night stand to be a mistake that "she would always regret?" That idea was no more palatable to Patrick than Annie cheating on him in the first place.

"Perhaps he was someone from the surgery?" Patrick said, returning to Annie's assault.

"If you mean a patient, no way. It's hard enough to believe Annie would screw someone she wasn't in love with. But a patient? Never happen. She had that Catholic guilt thing."

"Annie was raised Presbyterian."

"They're even worse. Some of them don't even drink." Daphne made a face to show that such a thing was inconceivable to her. "And I still don't get why she even told you. You would never have found out she slept with another bloke if she hadn't opened her trap." That statement reminded Patrick of Annie's comment: "Daphne has the morals of a feral cat."

"We made a promise to each other that we would not have other sexual partners. You know, STDs, HIV, etc." Patrick explained, bringing the topic down to a biological level Daphne could understand.

"That's why they invented condoms," Daphne said, accompanied by a look that said "duh." "Besides, no one keeps promises anymore."

"Yes, people *do* keep promises. That's why they're called 'promises' and not 'suggestions.'"

"Whatever," Daphne answered with a shrug.

Patrick stood up. This was getting him nowhere, and he was starting to get irritated. "Well, if you think of anything that would be helpful in the enquiry, please give me a ring." After buttoning his overcoat, he handed Daphne his card.

"Tell Annie I said 'hi.'"

"Tell her yourself. Annie always said no one could make her laugh like you did, and, right now, she could use a laugh."

"Maybe I'll do that."

"And lay off the pot. You're going to get caught." No comment from Daphne. "Don't say I didn't warn you." Turning up the collar on his coat, he went back into the cold.

* * *

Before leaving the station for the night, the desk sergeant handed Patrick a note from Annie. She had been discharged from the hospital and was going to stay with a friend. With his thumb, Patrick entered Annie's number into his mobile's directory and hit "talk."

"Hello, Patrick. I was hoping you wouldn't ring back," Annie said with a laugh in her voice.

"You're not that lucky."

"I've been released from the hospital, and I'm staying with a friend in Fulham."

"What friend?"

"Someone I know from the Harley clinic," Annie answered. "I chose not to take up any offers from the Sisterhood because they all have little ones at home. So when Connie said I could stay at her house for a couple days, I accepted. After hearing what you had to say about this attack being personal, I thought it best if I stayed with someone until I got my bearings straight. My head still hurts quite a bit."

"When you kiss a brick wall, you're head *will* hurt."

"True enough. About the locks at my flat, I was thinking about hiring a locksmith to redo the lock and put a chain on the door."

"Don't do that. I've got everything you need, including the locks." Actually, everything Patrick needed belonged to his dad who owned every tool ever made: saws, sockets, drills, and a box full of deadbolts. "Whenever B&Q has a half off sale, Dad is on it. As a result, he's changed every lock in his own house and my sisters as well at least twice. He keeps moving the locks around."

"How is your dad?"

Daniel Shea had recently undergone quadruple bypass surgery, and his rapid recovery had been declared a miracle by his wife and kids. Patrick knew Annie had been kept up to date on his father's progress by his sister Clare. Despite the breakup, she remained a family favourite, but would they have a different opinion of her if they knew the reason for the split?

"Tell your parents I said 'hello' when you see them," Annie said. "You *do* see them, don't you?"

"I can't talk right now," Patrick said, avoiding the question. He was already feeling guilty about not seeing his mother for nearly a month; he didn't need Annie to add to it. "But I have a few more thoughts on your assault."

"Patrick, I really don't…"

"I'll ring you later to see when it will be a good time to come over to change the locks." He folded his phone ending the call.

Chapter 10

Patrick spent the next day following up leads for a string of robberies in which stolen cars were driven into storefronts. While the driver backed out, his cohorts emptied the shop of its contents. They had a pretty good idea who was behind the rammings, but they had been unable to prove it. That had changed when Gwen Evans found CCTV footage giving a clear picture of the driver, Marjan Tomić, a member of a Croat gang that specialised in nicking cars.

After knocking on doors in Tomić's neighbourhood and finding that no one knew anything about anything, Patrick had contacted a snout who kept an eye on things for him, and he confirmed what he already suspected. Someone had tipped Tomić off about the video, and he had done a bunk. After talking with the uniforms who patrolled the neighbourhood, Patrick and Molly returned to the station.

By the time Patrick had finished his shift, it was after 8:00—a little late, but, perhaps, not too late to see Annie. Ever since the seed that her assailant might have been a fellow student had taken root, he had thought about little else. He decided to go ahead and ring her. *She can always say 'no.'*

"Patrick, I'm already in my pyjamas," Annie said, protesting the late visit.

"I've seen you in your pyjamas" *and out of them.* "Remember?"

"Yes, I remember." She felt a jolt go through her and wondered why she had ever let this man go.

"Where in Fulham does Connie live?" After giving him the street address, Patrick told her he could be there in fifteen minutes.

"You're coming from Hampden, and you'll be here in fifteen minutes? Did Father Christmas buy you a Ferrari or something that hovers above the traffic or pushes it out of the way?"

"Yes or no? May I come?"

"Okay, come ahead, but please do try not to scare the life out of me. You already have me on edge."

While riding the Underground to Fulham, Patrick thought about what he would say. As a result of the blow to her head, Annie hadn't heard what the attacker had whispered in her ear, so there was the possibility that whatever she had done to provoke the attack, she was still doing. In order to protect her, he would have to probe deeper into her personal and professional life.

Questioning a former lover would not be easy, but one of the first things taught at Hendon was to keep an emotional distance from the victim. Becoming personally involved could prove to be emotionally draining, or worse, it could jeopardise the case in the event it went to trial. The example given was of the detective who had slept with the victim of an assault. The barrister for her assailant had succeeded in getting the case thrown out of court because the cop's in-bed conversations with the victim had been deemed to be coaching, shaping her memory of the assault.

But Patrick's resolution to be the stoic detective went up in smoke as soon as Annie opened the door. Her head was still bandaged, and gauze covered the right side of her face. Her black eye now showed the first hints of that odd green that appeared when a bruise was healing. Evidence of her assault gave her the appearance of being vulnerable.

"What is it that you want to talk to me about?" Annie asked after directing Patrick to Connie's lounge.

"Thank you, yes, I'd love a cup of tea."

"I'll get it for you, luv," Connie said as she followed them into the lounge. "You go ahead with your visit."

"Do I know Connie?"

Patrick couldn't remember seeing her during his

86

visits to the Harley Street practice, but then he had rarely gone in. When he thought about how much money people spent on Botox and liposuction, it made him ill. If he managed to be in the neighbourhood at a time that coincided with Annie's lunch hour, they would usually meet at a nearby restaurant.

"I don't think so. Until recently, Connie split her time between the two offices. After I gave notice, she was offered a full-time position at Harley Street with Dr. Tranh."

"Can't say I'm sorry to hear you're out of there. A bunch of spoilt nobs with too much money in their pockets."

"I agree, but it was the only offer I got after university."

After a gentle tap on the lounge door, Connie entered with a set-up that would have pleased the queen, reminding Patrick of his grandmother's most cherished possession: a Royal Doulton tea service. After pouring out and a bit of chat, Connie left them alone. It was a school night, and Patrick and Annie could hear groans from Connie's kids after the dreaded word "homework" was bandied about.

Patrick began by telling Annie that he had driven by her house in Renwick. After leaving the South Hill estate, he had headed to Pullman Crescent. Even though the motorway separated Annie's neighbourhood from the housing estate, Annie's flat was still too close to the crumbling mass for Patrick's liking. Once the demolition teams had done their work in levelling the twin concrete towers, the whole of Hampden and Renwick would be safer because of it.

"The hedges are too high. It's a perfect place for an attacker to hide."

"I've already complained to Mr. Castle, my landlord," Annie said, as she settled into the settee, cup in hand. "He was, shall we say, less than receptive to my suggestion to hire someone to trim them, at least not before spring."

"I'll get Jack to do it. He owes me big time," Patrick said, while taking out his notebook. "Tell me about the layout."

Annie's flat was a typical converted two-story terrace house with an attic and shared entrance. On the ground floor was a flat occupied by the elderly Mr. Higgins, a retired postal worker. Annie's flat was on the first floor at the top of the stairs on the left and across the landing from a bedsit leased by Zafran Goh.

"Zafran's primary residence is in Singapore," Annie explained. "He was travelling so much to London that he decided to lease a bedsit rather than continue to pay the high rates at hotels. Even so, he's out of town more than he's in London. And it can't possibly be him because I think he's even shorter than I am, and my assailant wasn't that short. Besides, he is a sweet man. He lets me know by e-mail when he's coming back so I can air out his room, and he always brings me a little something from Singapore."

"Like what?"

"One time he brought me a brass urn to hold my ancestor's ashes. Not exactly a gift from someone who wants to woo you."

Annie's comment made Patrick think of his father's joke about an Irish proposal of marriage: "Mary, how would you like to be buried with my people?" Maybe in Singapore giving a girl a cremation urn was the ultimate romantic gesture, the equivalent of flowers in the West. It would be easy enough to check to see if Goh was in the country at the time of Annie's assault. Still, why would her neighbour want to punch her in the head?

"Back entrance?"

"Yes, but the garden's a sight," Annie answered. In years past, when tenants had moved out or were evicted, many of them had left their furnishings in the flat. The landlord's method of disposal had been to toss them into the garden. "Anyone trying to get into the house that way would most likely trip up on something. I don't go back there much. Even when we put out our rubbish, Mr. Higgins and I always use the front door, and Mr. Goh doesn't seem to generate any trash. I think he takes it to the office with him."

After writing everything down in his notebook, Patrick explained his theory that Annie might be the victim of a stalker from the university.

Annie started to laugh. "Patrick, this isn't like when you or I were at uni. These people are there to further their career goals with the costs picked up by their employers. It isn't about the lads picking up girls at the students' union. Besides, most of those taking the course are women."

"You're thinking too narrowly. It doesn't have to be someone taking the same course you are. On the nights you go to school, where do you go for dinner? Does anyone chat you up between courses? Did anyone offer to walk you to the bus stop, but you told him 'no?' What about going out for a drink? Things like that." Annie shook her head. "Don't just shake your head, Annie. You need to think about it for a minute."

"I don't have to think about it. I don't have dinner out because I eat a sandwich at my desk at work before leaving for the day. The only people who talk to me are women. No one has asked to drive me home or walk with me to the bus stop or take me for a drink. As I said, most of these people are there at the behest of their employers. They come right from work, and they can't wait to get home to their families. I am probably the youngest student taking the course."

When Annie continued to shake her head, dismissing all suggestions, Patrick decided it was time to get serious. He was convinced she still believed it was a random assault or a case of mistaken identity.

"I had my DC check your phone records. In the previous few weeks leading up to your assault, you had eight hang-up calls all from the same pay-as-you-go phone."

That statement got Annie's attention. "Why did you think it necessary to check my phone records?"

"Number one," Patrick said, holding up his index finger. "Although you and I are no longer romantically involved, I still care about you as a friend—a friend who was attacked. Number two. Although you insist this assault was not personal, everything I learnt at Hendon and on the job tells me this was a targeted attack. One of the easiest ways to get to know people and find patterns is by having a look at their phone records."

"Everyone gets hang-ups," Annie answered, but Patrick could hear the anxiety in her voice.

"Yes, but not from the same phone and not eight times."

"Patrick, you're frightening me."

"Good." Annie made a face. "When you're frightened, your body releases not only adrenalin, but also chemicals in the brain that may enhance your memory of the attack. Because it's been a few days since the assault and your wounds are healing, you might just remember something."

"All right. I promise to think about it."

"One more question. What the hell were you doing walking by yourself on Old School Road at 10:00 at night?"

"Oh, I neglected to tell you that I moonlight as a spy, and I was heading to a drop on the heath."

"What?"

"I'm kidding, Patrick. But, seriously, my chosen route is none of your business."

"John Stanley thinks you went that way in order to avoid paying a bus transfer." Patrick could tell from her face that Stanley had got it right. "Daphne told me your father cut off your allowance."

"Why on earth were you talking to Daphne? She's a total twit."

Patrick started to laugh. "*I* knew that. I just didn't know *you* did. I never understood why you let her stay at your flat."

"I let her stay *because* she's a twit. She's going to fumble along her whole life, so I thought that for a while, I might provide some stability. She's never had that. But you didn't answer my question. Why Daphne?"

"She might have noticed someone hanging about."

Annie shook her head. There was no way that was the real reason why Patrick had paid Daphne a visit.

"You still don't believe there has been no one since you and I broke up. But, I swear, it's true. I made a big...," but then she stopped. "We were talking about my route home."

"Yes, you said it was none of my business. But can it be my business to see that your locks get changed?"

"Yes. You can do that. I was planning to go home on Sunday. Does that work for you?"

"After six works. I have to go by my parents' house to pick up the lock."

"I'll see you then. And, please, no comments about the neighbourhood. It's what I can afford right now. Agreed?"

"Agreed."

Chapter 11

As soon as Patrick saw Gwen Evans's face, he knew he was in trouble. He just didn't know for what or with whom.

"Superintendent Craig would like to see you—immediately."

If the reason for the summons was that his wrist was going to be slapped, it could be a couple of things. Because of the time spent investigating Annie's attack, he hadn't filled out some of the endless forms required by modern police services and the one thing Craig was an absolute bear about or, and he really didn't want to think about this, Molly was in trouble for helping him on a case that rightly belonged to the Renwick station. He was working on a third possibility when Gwen interrupted him.

"You blew off the interview with *Global News*," she said in a whisper.

"Is that all?"

Gwen reminded him of the emphasis the super placed on cooperating with the press and shaped her fingers into the form of a triangle: community, press, police, that, according to Craig, formed the three legs of a stool needed for a safe community. Patrick disagreed with the second leg, especially when the newspaper involved was *Global News*. They were known for printing stories first, asking questions second, and publishing apologies third. With the best attorneys money could buy backing them up, they had a history of winning libel suits even if the story only had a slender thread of truth running through it.

"He's waiting for you," Gwen said, jerking her head in the direction of Craig's office. "Look sharp."

After putting on a tie he kept in his desk and running his hand through his thick hair, Patrick knocked on Craig's door. As usual, the man was wearing the regulation uniform of a superintendent. He believed, and rightly so, that the uniform and the hat with the chequered band screamed authority, confidence, and control. That was what the public expected from their police service, and from Craig, they got it.

Before sitting down, Patrick caught a glimpse of an edition of *Global News* on Craig's desk. So it really was about the missed telephone interview and had nothing to do with his investigation into Annie's assault.

After taking an offered chair, Patrick waited for the familiar lecture of participating, within reason, in a friendly collaboration with the Fourth Estate. As

Craig, preached the gospel of cooperation, he reiterated that the press should be viewed as allies and not adversaries in the fight against crime. Very much like a new convert, Craig proselytised about the tenets of his faith, in this case, having the press do some of the work for you.

"We don't want to get on the wrong side of *Global News*, now do we? They are the newspaper of choice for the common man. That is where Mr. Average gets most of his news."

Patrick disagreed. In his opinion, most people got their news from the telly or the internet. People read *Global News* for the scandals of the rich and famous and for the topless women on page three. It was only people who were fifty or older who actually bought a newspaper.

"I'm sorry, sir, if this caused you any inconvenience. When the reporter called, I was out on the South Hill estate looking for the missing Dorsett girl. My first priority was to make sure Tanya Dorsett was safe."

"Perfectly understandable, Patrick," Craig said, nodding in agreement, and it appeared that he meant it. "By the way, kudos for a quick result in the Dorsett matter. I think you should mention that in your interview this morning with Patricia Gresham, the reporter from *Global News*."

"This morning, sir? But DC Updike and I are

trying to track down the suspect in the ramming cases. We have some good leads."

"I intend to assign that enquiry to Prentiss and Dillon."

"Sir, but I have *my* informants looking…"

"Miss Gresham should be here in about ten minutes," Craig said, looking at his watch. "She's very keen to have the interview run in the Hampden section this weekend. Of course, her primary focus will be on your nicking the Hampden Burglar."

As if on cue, the phone rang indicating Miss Gresham was at the front desk waiting to interview Patrick.

"Remember, whatever you say you are saying on behalf of the whole Hampden station. In fact, allow me to go a step further. You are representing the Metropolitan Police. We are counting on you, DS Shea. But I know you won't disappoint. You have a brilliant future ahead of you. You've been fast-tracked for a reason. Don't muck it up."

Showing considerable restraint by not saluting and clicking his heels, Patrick went to meet Miss Gresham.

* * *

Patrick was already familiar with Patricia Gresham's work. In addition to being a reporter, she had a column called "On the Beat," in which she wrote about police work conducted at street level, mostly by uniformed cops who appreciated the attention. It was the detectives who gave her a wide berth. They found her enquiries to be intrusive, and in some cases, felt she had prematurely released details of a crime that should have remained under wraps. As far as he knew, she had never once darkened the door of the Hampden nick, preferring to focus her attention on high-profile murders and crimes of passion. He couldn't imagine her interest in anything as mundane as the Hampden Burglar.

With the office abuzz with the sounds of computers and phones and traded barbs between coppers, Miss Gresham was waiting for Patrick in an interview room sequestered from the drone of a police station. As soon as he set eyes on Patricia Gresham, he thought he had been set up.

"This is a joke, right?" Patrick said as soon as he had closed the door.

"Hello, Patrick It's been awhile."

Patricia Gresham was actually Patty Gilhooley, who had grown up three houses down from the Shea residence in Kilburn, and his first serious crush.

"Honestly, when I rang the station requesting an interview, I didn't know it was you. Believe it or not, you are not the only Patrick Shea in London."

"Too right," Patrick said, acknowledging a common Irish surname, especially in Kilburn where his father had six brothers, and every one of them had a son named Patrick which was why, when his mother talked about him with the relatives, she always referred to him as "our Patrick."

"I didn't know it was *my* Patrick Shea until your secretary faxed your picture to my office. As for my *nom de plume*, Patricia Gresham sounds a lot better than Patty Gilhooley."

He wanted to add that the alias also spared the Gilhooley family a lot of embarrassment considering the tripe Patty wrote under her byline.

Before getting down to business, Patty and Patrick took turns updating each other on their respective families. While the Sheas remained firmly entrenched in the most Irish of London villages, the Gilhooleys had left Kilburn for the manicured lawns of Hampshire a dozen years earlier. After university and a degree in journalism, Patty had taken a job in Japan working in an English-language programme designed to train the Japanese in the art of writing blog posts. After an internship at a newspaper in Bristol, she had landed the beat reporter job with *Global News*. It probably didn't hurt that she was a drop-dead gorgeous redhead and looked good in a skirt. With her perfume filling the air, he imagined there were few cops who could resist her charms, but he was one of them.

"I understand your marriage didn't take,"

Gresham began. Patrick nodded, but offered no details. "So how does it feel to be a bachelor once again?"

"I'm married to the job now."

Gresham looked sceptical. Patrick was a fine looking man with eyes that could make a girl melt and someone who kept himself fit. Although a little on the short side, his lack of height did not translate into a lack of length, and she smiled at the memory of their times together.

"Honest to God," he said, raising his hand as if swearing an oath. "I'm not in a relationship with anyone." For a moment, he thought about Annie, completely skipping over Susan, a sure sign that it was time to pull the plug.

"I'm married to my job as well, but I do have to eat," Patricia purred, and then hopped up on the interview table, her legs dangling over the side. "Why don't we reminisce about all the good times we had in Kilburn while eating lunch, or if you can stretch your lunch hour out, my flat's only fifteen minutes from here?"

"You're not seriously going through with this interview." Gresham just smiled. "You and I have a history."

"Is that what they call it now—a history? I thought we had sex."

Patrick had very fond memories of Patty

Gilhooley. She had been his first: his first kiss, his first feel, his first time going all the way. For a Catholic-school girl, she was delightfully uninhibited, and she knew a lot more about the subject than he did. She had planned his deflowering with military precision: time, place, date. It was she who had the presence of mind to bring the condoms. But looking at her now, with her short skirt and long legs, he had the feeling he was being lured into a spider web. It was a well-known fact that *Global News* had cops on the payroll at every police station in the Metropolitan Police and at Scotland Yard as well, but he had no intention of becoming one of her sources, no matter how generous, or tempting, the offer.

"Conflict of interest here, Patty."

"Patricia, please. Patty Gilhooley will remain forever in Kilburn," she said, tapping his hand with a long red fingernail. "If on the off chance someone finds out we know each other, they will not have learnt it from me."

Because Patrick believed the arrest of the Hampden Burglar was a flash-in-the-plan story, he decided to go ahead with the interview. After hearing the details, Patty would probably shelve the story. It wasn't exactly a rip roaring tale of derring-do. But instead of putting her off, she saw it as the perfect contrast to the newspaper's usual stories of blood and gore. She insisted her editor would love it.

"If you actually print this story, I want you to mention Detective Constable Molly Updike. She's my partner, and she covers my back. She was there when we nicked Jacobs."

"But the burglar didn't hand DC Updike a rose, now did he?"

"So you know about that?" Patrick asked, the muscles in his jaw tightening, "which means you've already talked to someone here at the station. Why don't you do an interview with them? Tell my mates I sent you." And he stood up and walked to the door. It seemed he had been set up after all—most likely by the station's clowns, Prentiss and Dillon.

"Sit down, Patrick, and listen to me," Gresham said, pointing to the vacated chair, but Patrick waved her off. "Ever since September 11, people are seeing evildoers everywhere, so it will be a relief to read a story where no one got hurt. You should look at this as community outreach to the citizens of Hampden. Let the public read about their police force doing their job and doing it well. That is certainly Superintendent Craig's take on it."

With Craig in mind, he agreed to do the interview. But as soon as they had finished, he opened the door indicating they were done. "Now that you've got what you want, I had better get back to my job of protecting the community. It was good seeing you."

"Thanks for talking to me, Patrick," Gresham

said, squeezing past him. "By the way, the offer stands about getting together. If you change your mind, be sure to bring the handcuffs."

Chapter 12

Annie's flat was in a section of Renwick best described as shabbily genteel. Her flat was in a terrace house that had been built in the late 1950s when there was still a critical shortage of housing as a result of the widespread bombing of London during the Second World War, and shortcuts were taken. Despite its lower middle class orientation, most houses were fronted with neat patches of lawn. Many of the residents had repainted the doors and window frames sometime within the last five years, and almost every entrance sported a terra cotta flower pot or window box that in the spring would be bursting with the blooms of the season.

Armed with his father's toolbox, Patrick approached Annie's flat with a professional eye. If he were a security advisor, he would have told her that the lock on the front door needed to be changed as it would take a thief less than a minute to pick it with tools used by Fagin's gang of lads in the mid eighteenth century. But without the landlord's approval, there was nothing he could do about it.

Before going up the stairs to her flat, Patrick had a look around. On the ground floor, there was a storage closet under the stairs leading to the first floor, but when he opened it, he found it chock full of junk. If someone wanted to hide in there, he'd have to clean it out first. There was also a door leading to the garden that had a chain on it and a better lock than that on the front door. Patrick threw the switch for the floodlights, and as Annie had mentioned, it looked more like a scrapyard than a back garden with a narrow path cutting through the detritus to a shared fence and gate with a neighbour on the next street.

On the landing Annie shared with Mr. Goh, there was a staircase leading to a storage area in the attics. If someone were to sit high up on the stairs, Annie would not see him. After picking the lock on the front door, someone could lay in wait. It was a set up for an assault in the making.

Then there was the door to Annie's flat. When the single-family house had been converted to three separate dwellings, the owner had not bothered to upgrade the doors from standard interior to something that would provide the tenants with more security. A strong shoulder or a good kick could easily knock in Annie's door. Patrick was pretty sure it was a code violation, but going that route would take time. He was trying to remember if his father had a better door in his garage when Annie opened the door. He was pleased to see that most of the bandages had been removed. She was starting to look like *his* Annie.

Without preamble, he asked why the front entrance was unlocked.

"Because I knew you were coming."

"That shouldn't matter. You should always keep it locked."

Annie explained that Mr. Higgins on the ground floor was in his seventies, and his daughters and grandchildren frequently stopped by. It was easier for him if the front door remained unlocked, but Patrick wasn't having it.

"Isn't your safety worth more than their convenience?"

Patrick didn't bother to apologise for being so abrupt. Annie understood that if something was amiss, he was like a hound on the scent, and something was definitely wrong with this picture.

"I'm sure I can get you a stronger door. My Dad's semi-retired now. To keep him out of my mum's hair, he spends his time going to jumble and estate sales and sells his loot on the internet. He's got a nice little business going."

"Well, there's no need for us to have this conversation on the landing," Annie said, making way for Patrick to come in and offered to make him dinner. "I can cook up some eggs and sausage with a tomato."

"Lovely."

While Annie saw to dinner, Patrick had a look around. It didn't take long. The flat was tight quarters with a small kitchen and an even smaller bath and shower. In the living area, there was only room enough for a couch, chair, end table, and a small TV propped up on a wooden cube, an IKEA special. Obviously, her father's decision to stop Annie's allowance had really hurt her, and he wondered if Mr. Jameson had any idea of just how far Annie had fallen or if he even knew about her assault. It would be just like her not to tell him so he wouldn't worry.

"Your sink is dripping," Patrick called out to her. As the son of a plumber, if there was one thing that made him crazy, it was leaks. If he couldn't take care of it, he would ring his dad, a man whose mission in life was to leave no leak unplugged. "After we eat, I can fix that as well."

"So you did learn something from your old man," Annie said, leaning against the door of the bathroom. When she had first met Patrick, he had told her that in the Shea family, everyone had to choose a profession from one of three disciplines, all beginning with the letter "p": plumber, priest, or policeman. Because of the disgusting stories his dad told about what people threw down their toilet, he did not want to be a plumber. With that occupation crossed off the list, only the police force and the priesthood remained. For all of a second, Annie thought Patrick had seriously contemplated becoming a priest, but then he had smiled at her. There was no way a handsome, straight man with a smile like that was ever going to remain celibate. The irony of his choosing to become a cop was that a murder scene was more disgusting than anything his father had ever fished out of a toilet.

As soon as they were seated, Annie brought up Patrick's favourite subject: Josh Shea. She absolutely adored Patrick's son. The boy was well behaved, polite, and, like his father, easy to entertain. All you had to do was to produce a football, and he was happy. Annie had never felt that Josh was an intrusion into their personal life. If things had worked out with his dad, she would have loved being his stepmom.

"He's such a good kid," Patrick said, beaming. "Like I told you, he's at St. Edmund's now, and he's holding his own against all those rich kids, and not just in football, but in academics as well."

"That shouldn't surprise you. He has a curious mind and was always asking questions."

"He asks after you."

"Really?" Annie was surprised, but pleased. "Maybe we could get together at some point. I'd love to see him."

"I don't see why not. We could all go to a match when Chelsea plays Arsenal."

For the first time, Patrick looked directly at Annie. The sounds of her cooking in the kitchen had stirred up a lot of memories. When they had been together, Annie often cooked. She was one of those people who could make scrambled eggs interesting. While working her culinary magic, Patrick would tell her about his day, leaving out any bits she might find alarming. She was a good listener and seemed interested in his stories. After dinner, she would take one corner of the couch so that she could prop up her book on its arm, and he would put his head in her lap. As she read, she would run her fingers through his hair, but as they got closer to calling it a night, she would unbutton his shirt with her free hand. Upon reaching the button above his belt, she would close the book, indicating that it was time for bed and making love. They usually began with him lying on his belly. Annie would straddle him and rub his back until he was so relaxed that he was in danger of nodding off, but that's when their lovemaking would begin in earnest. It had all been going so well until...

"Well, I better get after it," Patrick said, shaking his head to dislodge the memory. "I'm going to start with changing out the lock and putting a chain on the door. That's my number one priority."

While Patrick replaced the lock and fixed the plumbing, Annie served as his assistant, handing him his tools and asking about his prospects for a transfer to Scotland Yard and a murder investigation team. Although she admired him for the work he did, she had always disliked his profession, one requiring that he deal with the very worst in society on a daily basis. She had never understood why *anyone* would want the job, especially someone as lovely as Patrick.

"Well, that should do it," he said, closing the lid on his toolbox. "All it needed was a new washer. No more drip." When he stood up, he was less than a foot away from Annie.

"Aren't you forgetting something?" Puzzled, Patrick shook his head. "Your tool?" With her scent overwhelming him, at the moment, he could think of only one tool. "Your spanner. It's under the sink."

"Oh that. Got it," he said, picking up the stray tool and depositing in the box. "What's this?" Patrick asked, pointing to a deep cut near her right eye. Previously bandaged, it was the first time he was seeing it.

"That's where my assailant punched me."

"You said he was wearing gloves." Annie nodded. "The ring must have had a raised setting to gouge you like that."

"I'm pretty sure it's going to leave a scar, but if that's the worst of it, I can live with it."

"A small scar won't change how beautiful you are." With alarms going off in his jeans, he squeezed past her. "I'll ring my dad to see if he has a better door, and you need to ask your landlord if I can replace the lock on the front door. Tell him that a friend of yours, who happens to be a policeman, strongly suggests you do it. I'll take care of getting the extra keys made for the other residents."

"I appreciate your concern, but you always told me that if someone really wanted to break into a house they'd find a way."

"Yes, that's mostly true. But the more difficult you make it for him, the more time it takes and that increases your chances of having the police get to the site before he runs off with your valuables. In thwarting a criminal, time is of the essence."

"Any burglar would be disappointed. I don't have any valuables."

"Sometimes that's worse. It only makes them angry, and they..."

"Goodnight, Patrick," she said, pushing him out the door.

Chapter 13

With a cold front stalled over most of England, the frigid temperatures continued to keep everyone indoors, including the criminals, and there was a decrease in all crime categories except domestic violence, the result of too many unhappy couples being forced to spend time together indoors. Familiarity bred not only contempt, but violence. The result was that the usual frenzy of the Hampden station had been replaced by a welcomed lull, welcomed, that is, by everyone except Superintendent Craig, who scheduled a meeting to discuss re-activating cold-case files.

Patrick and Molly were handed a slim file concerning the death of Simon Anderson: white male, seventy-seven years old, whose death was a result of a drug overdose of legally prescribed medications. In the end, the coroner had ruled the death to be an accidental overdose, and no further action was taken.

The reason the case had been pulled for review was that in the seven months since Mr. Anderson's death, a civil action had been filed on behalf of his two former stepdaughters claiming wrongful death as a result of negligence on the part of the daughter, Phyllis Langford. From a policeman's point of view, there was always the possibility that, during the discovery phase, something new had been uncovered that might warrant a second look. But Patrick and Molly knew the most likely reason for the review was that the stepdaughters or their mother had friends in high places, and word had come down from above to take another look at the case. There was a lot at stake: an inheritance of nearly a half million pounds and several properties whose value doubled the bottom line.

Follow-up could easily have been done by telephone, but if Patrick and Molly remained at their desks, it was likely Craig would find something else for them to do that might require their being outside knocking on doors. With temperatures well below freezing, it was an easy call, and they headed out to see Carl Dudley, Esq.

As a copper, Patrick didn't like lawyers. He saw them as people employed in the business of delay and obfuscation. He particularly disliked barristers whose job it was to take legitimate police actions and turn them into a violation of their clients' civil rights. To them, cross-examination was not the search for the truth, but a contest of adversaries where witnesses, including police officers, were the pawns. Was it any wonder that witnesses were scarce when coppers came looking for help in solving a crime?

Mr. Dudley's offices were on High Street in Renwick, an area that had been designated by an economics foundation as "offering identikit shopping with little local character." True enough, Patrick thought, as Molly and he entered a drab two-story stucco building next to a Chinese takeaway. The interior was the very definition of the word "bland," and the reception-room chairs looked like they had been ordered from an office catalogue for start-ups.

After identifying themselves to Dudley's receptionist, the two were immediately led into the solicitor's office. The room looked little different from the generic reception room. The impression Dudley wanted to make was that here was a professional who wasn't going to waste your money on a wood-panelled office with overstuffed leather chairs and a silver tea set. He was going to put your fees to work for *you*. But Patrick suspected that a Jaguar, parked in a space easily seen from the solicitor's office, belonged to Dudley. If so, the bloke was doing all right.

After an exchange of pleasantries, Dudley, who was thirty-something and as plain as the furnishings in his office, stated that it was an encouraging sign to see that the police were having a second look at the case. It was his hope that they were bringing something new to him, not the other way around.

"No, the police don't have anything new. We are merely conducting a routine review of the file," Patrick began, pleased to see Dudley's hopes that something incriminating had been found go up in smoke. "Occasionally, the discovery process in a civil suit will shed some light on a case."

"Sorry to disappoint, DS Shea. There is nothing new here either, but it's not necessary. We are confident that the known facts will result in a reversal of the decision made by the probate court."

Patrick looked sceptical. Before leaving the station, Molly and he had spent an hour going through the file. As far as they could tell, there was nothing there. Noting his look, Dudley explained to the officers that the burden of proof in a civil suit was less onerous than that in a criminal case.

"Is that right?" Patrick answered. "That's good to know. I'll have to write that down."

"The fact is Phyllis Anderson Langford refused all offers of help by my clients for the care of her elderly father and insisted that all medical decisions be left to her and to her alone," Dudley said, ignoring the sarcasm. "It is our contention that Mrs. Langford failed in her duty of care in protecting her father from overdosing on his medications."

"In other words, through Mrs. Langford's negligence, Simon Anderson ingested a lethal dose of prescription medicine. Have I got that right?"

"Exactly. At the time the prescriptions were filled, Mrs. Langford made a specific request to the chemist, Mr. Sanjay Patel at the All-Drug in Hampden, that her father's medication not be placed in tamper-proof bottles, claiming she suffered from arthritis thereby making it difficult for her to open them."

"That's not an uncommon request by arthritis sufferers or the elderly."

"True. Which is why we have asked Mrs. Langford to submit to a physical examination for the purpose of determining the severity of her arthritis. She has declined to do so."

"According to the medical report, Mr. Anderson had a stroke six months before his death," Patrick said, referring to his notes in the notebook balanced on his knee. "As a result, it became necessary for him to use a wheelchair, and he was no longer able to care for himself. It was also noted in the file that he was taking anti-depressants. Is it possible Mr. Anderson was unable to accept these changes and took his own life?"

Patrick knew the solicitor would never acknowledge such a possibility. If Simon Anderson's death was ruled a suicide, his insurance company would most likely refuse to pay out on the policy, but he wanted to see how high Dudley would jump. As it turned out, pretty high.

"Absolutely not!" the outraged solicitor answered.

"Yes, it is true Mr. Anderson had suffered a stroke, but his cognition was relatively unaffected. In the last six months of his life, he made decisions regarding the sale of his business and several properties. According to his stepdaughters, who loved him dearly and whose affection was returned by Mr. Anderson, he was occasionally, but not chronically, depressed. Although things changed because of the stroke, his will to live remained strong."

"Were the stepdaughters excluded from the will?"

"No, but the amount they received is a pittance compared to Mrs. Langford's inheritance."

"If they were so dear to him, why leave them only a pittance?"

"It seems Mr. Anderson suffered from a lingering sense of guilt as a result of his divorce from the first Mrs. Anderson because, a year after the divorce was finalised, she died of breast cancer. Mrs. Langford was their only child."

"Although the stepdaughters might not like how Mr. Anderson chose to assuage his guilt over the divorce from the first Mrs. Anderson, it was his right to leave them only a pittance."

"That is for a jury to decide, DS Shea. Is there anything else I can help you with?"

* * *

"I wonder if all this would go away if Mrs. Langford

would just give the stepdaughters a bigger share of the money?" Molly asked as soon as they were back in the car.

"I can almost guarantee it. I'm sure the only reason the daughter is digging in is because she thinks the stepdaughters don't have a case. Tell me again what we know about the stepdaughters."

Molly flipped open a copy of the file that included Xeroxed copies of photos of Lorraine Ludlow and Donna Perrine, two attractive blondes, both in their late twenties, which meant that they were about twenty years younger than Phyllis Langford, the heir to the Anderson fortune and his properties. On a second page was a photo of their mother, the second Mrs. Anderson, an attractive woman in her fifties wearing enough jewellery to keep Tiffany & Co. in business. From the date on the picture, it appeared that although their marriage had ended in divorce, Mr. Anderson and his former wife continued to make the rounds of London society giving all the appearances of being a happily married couple.

"Both Ludlow and Perrine are married to partners in Weldon Enterprises," Molly said, flipping back to the pages referencing the stepdaughters.

"Really? Weldon owns most of the construction cranes used in high-rise buildings. Any building with more than six stories has a Weldon crane on it."

"In other words, the stepdaughters should have

enough money on their own without dipping their fingers into Phyllis Langford's till."

"For most people, there is no such thing as enough money," Patrick said, turning the key of the BMW. "Let's see if Mrs. Langford is in the mood to talk."

* * *

The address in the file for Phyllis Langford was in Hampden's wealthiest neighbourhood, a section of detached homes leaning heavily in favour of half-timbered, Tudor-style residences. In the driveway was a highly-polished black 2000 Lexus sitting next to an aging Land Rover with mud on its tires. A stone path bisected an immaculate lawn leading to a double door with leaded glass panes. It was exactly what one would expect to find in the posh Black Forest section of Hampden.

"When I was a kid, I pretended that I lived in a neighbourhood just like this," Molly said, admiring the house and garden.

"Really? I always imagined living in a duplex in Wimbledon," Patrick said, thinking about the eight people stuffed into the Shea Victorian terrace house in Kilburn.

"That's because you're basically a shanty Irishman," Molly said, laughing. "You probably consider a six-pack of beer and a baked potato to be a seven-course meal."

"You need to get some new jokes, Molly," Patrick said in a disapproving tone. "My grandfather told me that one when he handed me my first bottle of Guinness."

"When was that? Your First Holy Communion?"

"Oh, come on! I was only seven when I received communion. No, I didn't get my first taste until much later—at my Confirmation—when I was twelve," Patrick said, smiling as he remembered slurping the foam off his Gramps' glass of stout and everyone laughing at his cream-colored moustache.

All banter ceased when, through the leaded glass, Patrick and Molly could see a wavy form making its way to the front door.

"I have nothing new to add to the statement I made to the police back in April," Phyllis Langford said, as she led the officers down a long hallway to a study. "I want you to understand that the only reason I agreed to this interview is that the solicitor representing the stepsisters will make hay of it if I don't." She gestured for Patrick and Molly to have a seat in two oversized leather chairs that made Patrick want to reach for a pipe and his paper and ring for Jeeves. No refreshments were offered.

Phyllis Langford was an attractive woman in her early fifties, dressed in a simple but well-tailored two-piece grey suit. Apparently, the loss of her father and the subsequent legal imbroglio had taken its toll as she had circles under her eyes, and her jacket appeared to be a size too large for her.

"I know why you are here," Mrs. Langford began. "My father's former stepdaughters have filed a lawsuit in the hopes of gaining, at the very least, a greater share of the inheritance left to me by my father. My solicitor has informed me that I have been accused of wilful negligence in relation to my father's death. You want to find out if I am guilty."

After scooting forward on a chair that had been engulfing her, Molly explained in a voice that someone would use in comforting a grieving relation that it was true that the lawsuit had triggered a review of the file. "However, the reason we are here is to clarify a few things."

Patrick had encouraged Molly to take the lead in the interview. He suggested she adopt the role of confidante in the hopes of forming a bond with Langford. But he wasn't sure it would work. Mrs. Langford looked as if she was prepared to do battle.

"It's about those damn safety caps, isn't it?"

Molly nodded. "We spoke with Mr. Dudley, the solicitor for…"

"Oh, I know who Mr. Dudley is."

"Mr. Dudley told us that, at your request, the tamper-proof caps were not used on your father's prescriptions and that you refused to submit to a physical exam that would substantiate your claims that you suffered from arthritis."

"Well, he got it half right," Mrs. Langford said with acid dripping from her tongue. "If you look at my hands, you will see I suffer from mild arthritis as many people in their fifties do," she said, holding her hands out for their inspection. "The problem is not the arthritis; it is that I have no strength in my hands. I can't get the damn things off the bottles. If you were to examine my own medical cupboard, you will find that none of my medications have safety caps on them. Because my own children are grown, it is no longer necessary as I do not have grandchildren. As for Donna and Lorraine's children, they were never here. My father had a very low tolerance for young children. They were rarely to be seen and never heard."

"Is there any possibility your father deliberately took a lethal dose of medication?" Molly asked.

"I can't answer that question. I really can't," Mrs. Langford said with a sadness seeping into her voice. "And it's not as if I haven't thought about it. All his life, my father was an active man. He hunted and fished. He was an enthusiastic fossil hunter and travelled the world in pursuit of them. When in the country, he rode his bicycle into the village every morning to buy the newspaper. After his stroke, he found he could do none of those things, and he became depressed. In his misery, he wanted to be left alone. He didn't want to see anyone, including me. The only time I was allowed into his suite of rooms was to see that he took his medications and to serve him his meals."

"Were you his sole caregiver?"

Mrs. Langford shook her head. "Three times a week, he was visited by Mrs. Atwater, a nurse from Medico UK. She told me that because Daddy was so rude to her that if it weren't for me, she would not have kept him as a client. Of course, she understood his behaviour was because of his frustration with his medical condition, but knowing that doesn't make it any easier to have someone railing at you in incoherent rants. He was never the easiest of men, but the stroke... It just made him even more so."

While Mrs. Langford shared with Molly a typical day caring for an active man trapped inside the body of an invalid, Patrick watched the daughter. She was making no claim, as were the stepdaughters, to having been a beloved daughter who deserved all of the money her father had left her. But like so many children, whose parents were unworthy of their love, she *did* love him, and his gut told him that there was no way she would have assisted in his death. She was clearly grieving.

"What can you tell us about Mrs. Ludlow and Mrs. Perrine?"

"Oh, yes, the much aggrieved stepdaughters.

Although my father couldn't stand them, he liked their mother very much, as did I, or as much as a daughter can like her father's mistress. But the only way Daddy could have the mother without the daughters was to divorce Louise, and he did that three years ago. In the divorce, Louise received a generous settlement with the understanding that she would get nothing from him in his will, and she agreed. To keep the daughters from circling, my father settled a lump sum amount of £20,000 on each, allowing him to say truthfully that they were in his will because, believe me, they *did* ask. But with the way they go through money, it's not enough. If they got everything, in the end, it wouldn't be enough."

"I understand they are married to partners in Weldon Enterprises."

Mrs. Langford nodded. "My father was good friends with Martin Weldon and was able to secure positions for both of their husbands. They are unexceptional men with exceedingly poor taste in women, but they are handsome and that is all that matters to Donna and Lorraine."

"Was there any problem with the insurance company regarding the payout on your father's life insurance policies?" Molly asked.

"No. Mrs. Atwater, Daddy's caregiver, signed a sworn affidavit that on the day my father died he was particularly confused. By the time she had finished her ministrations…"

"What did they include?"

"Bathing, clipping his nails, brushing his teeth, very personal things that he did not want me to do. Because we had the bathroom redone after the stroke to accommodate his needs, he was able to use the toilet without assistance, but bathing was quite beyond his capabilities."

"Where were the medicines stored?"

"They were lined up on his vanity in the bathroom. When I found my father, the medicine bottles were all open, and pills were everywhere, including aspirin, vitamins, and antacids. The autopsy showed that he took a little bit of everything—just shoving them in his mouth without any consideration as to what they were."

"Well, I think we've got everything we need," Molly said, closing her notebook. "We need not trouble you any further."

In a soft voice, Mrs. Langford asked for them to remain. Apparently, Molly had succeeded in establishing a rapport with the grieving daughter.

"There *is* a reason why I do not think my father committed suicide. Many years ago, Daddy was the plaintiff in a lawsuit regarding a real estate scheme in Cornwall. The suit went on for more than a year, and he incurred huge legal costs. As a result, he developed a profound distrust for all solicitors, including his own. Daddy would have known that any suspicion that his death was a suicide would lead to a legal challenge. He thought by including Donna and Lorraine in the will he had got 'round that. But he had failed to gauge the depth of their greed." Shaking her head, she added, "They cared nothing for him— nothing. To them, he was a deep pocket and nothing more."

"May I make a suggestion, Mrs. Langford?" Patrick asked as they walked to the front door. "Go to a doctor and get a strength test done."

* * *

"This is crap," Molly said as they walked to the car.

"You don't believe Mrs. Langford's story?" Patrick would be surprised if she didn't. Molly was worse than a pit bull if she thought someone was lying to her, but Mrs. Langford had basically cruised.

"Of course I believe her! The only reason we're here is because Cinderella's stepsisters got their mother to ring her MP. I can just hear it. 'Oh, Chauncey, please do ring Superintendent Craig and see what can be done to help my darlings,'" Molly said in a high-pitch squeal. "The next thing you know, boom! The file gets pulled for review. I hope those evil sisters lose in court and have to pay Mrs. Langford's legal fees."

"I hope they lose as well. But 'Chauncey?' Is that your idea of a toff's name?"

"Stuff it, Shea!"

"Chauncey? Seriously?"

"If you don't shut up, I won't type up your notes on the Annie Jameson case."

Patrick pretended to zip his lips and throw away the key. No one could organise notes like Molly, and he wanted to take the file home with him. He was hoping that something from his interviews with Annie and Daphne Pierson would jump out at him. If it didn't, then it was case closed.

Chapter 14

The whole thing with Phyllis Langford had left a bad taste in Patrick's mouth. Other than the request for a non-tamperproof cap on the medicine bottles, there wasn't a scintilla of evidence to support the stepdaughters' assertion that Langford had been negligent in the care of her father. The coroner's report supported the details provided by Langford as to the events on the day her father had died, and a telephone call to the agency nurse backed up Langford's story as well. According to Nurse Atwater, Mrs. Langford believed that as long as her father's cognitive abilities remained largely intact, his was a life worth living. Statements from friends showed a daughter who was doing everything she could to keep her father alive. The case should never have been reopened.

The scene of a daughter grieving for her father and Annie being kept at arm's length by her dad because of his remarriage prompted a telephone call to Josh. Although most of the boy's responses were 'yes,' or 'dunno,' Patrick loved talking to his son.

Josh finally found his voice when he reminded his dad that Ally had given her approval to his getting a Gameboy for Christmas.

"Duly noted, Josh."

"Is that copper talk for 'yes'?"

"It's not up to me, now is it? Father Christmas is the one who decides."

"Hmm."

"I ran into an old friend of yours—Annie Jameson," Patrick said, changing the subject. He didn't particularly like his son's answer. Shouldn't an eight-year-old boy still believe in Father Christmas? "She said to say 'hi' and that Chelsea would kick Arsenal's butt."

"Never happen! She doesn't know what she's talking about," the boy shouted into the phone, but immediately quieted down. "Are you going to start seeing her again?"

"Dunno," he answered, mimicking his son.

"What kind of answer is that?" Josh said, aping his father. "Hold on. Mum wants to talk to you?"

Because Patrick could hear Ally shooing Josh out of the room, he knew the conversation was going to be about the Gameboy, the #1 gift on his son's Christmas wish list.

"Yes, I got the Gameboy. I even wrapped it." Actually, the electronics store had wrapped it, but he didn't need to tell her that. "I'm surprised you caved."

"I didn't cave," Ally said defensively. "The deal was that Josh had to excel in all his classes, which he did. You'll have to get it to me early. We leave for France on the 22nd. Any problem with that?"

"No. I'll ring you before I come over."

"Why don't you come to dinner? We haven't talked in a long time."

Whenever Ally invited him to dinner, it was usually because she was on a fishing expedition about his personal life. He knew from conversations with her husband, who was very open about what went on in their marriage, that Ally continued to experience guilt over their divorce. Even though Ally had known from day one that Patrick would be joining the police service, the reason for the split was because she couldn't deal with the realities of his chosen profession. Until Patrick had settled down with a nice girl, someone who would be a good stepmom to Josh, Ally would continue to probe.

"I know what this is about. Clare rang you and told you about Annie."

On average, Patrick spoke with his oldest sister about twice a week. Through Clare, he could keep his parents up to date on Jack and he would be kept abreast of what was happening in the Shea clan. Clare was the equivalent of the top of the hour news wrap-up: family news in ten minutes or less.

"Annie? Annie who?"

"Give it up, Ally. You're talking to a detective. Just tell me what it is you want to know."

"To start with, is Annie all right?"

Rather than answering a string of questions, Patrick divulged the whole of the story and brought Ally up to date on the current state of the enquiry, that is, if you could call conducting one interview with a former flat mate and a check of Annie's phone records an enquiry.

"Are you going to start dating her again?"

"Actually, I've been thinking about it. But I can't get past the fact that Annie cheated on me. It just gnaws at me. Here I was out looking at engagement rings, and she's screwing some bloke she insists she never saw again. How could I ever trust her?"

"Patrick, everyone deserves a second chance."

Considering that Ally had been the one to end their marriage, refusing to give *him* a second chance, it was an odd statement to make, but he kept quiet. No sense in digging around in old rubbish.

"Don't decide this on your own. Talk to Annie about it," Ally continued. "Maybe it was hormonal. She had a rush of testosterone, just like men get and couldn't control herself."

"Women have testosterone? I didn't know that." But Allison *would* know. She was a health fanatic who got her information from reading medical journals. She ran two miles every day and was a culinary crusader preaching the gospel of plant-based protein. Because meat and pork had been banished from her kitchen soon after her marriage to the go-along-to-get-along Peter Petrie, Josh found it necessary to phone his dad asking for emergency visits so that they could go out and have a hamburger or a meat pie together.

As far as *his* testosterone levels were concerned, after being in such close proximity to Annie, Patrick knew they were elevated. He had wanted to take Annie right there in that little bathroom. Bang her up against the door and have at it.

"There's another problem with me and Annie getting back together. She didn't like me being a copper any better than you did. That's not going to change."

"That's true. But at least give her the option of saying 'no.'"

"Well, first things first. I have to find a way to end things with Susan. I've been trying, but it hasn't been going well."

Ally's advice with regard to Susan was to just get it over with. In her opinion, there was no such thing as cushioning the blow of someone telling you that a relationship had run its course. That was certainly the way Ally had handled the end of their marriage.

132

While he had been away for a three-day course for the job, Ally had hired a divorce attorney and hit him with the bad news almost as soon as he had entered their flat. He had known things were not going smoothly, but he had never for one minute thought it would end up in divorce court. That evening, he had gone on a bender with his mates. After sobering up, he started thinking about his future without Ally and Josh. It had been the lowest point in his life.

"I hope you do get back with Annie," Ally continued, interrupting his thoughts, "because Josh really likes her. It's not that he dislikes Susan, but to quote your son, 'Annie does stuff with me.'"

"I'll take it under advisement."

* * *

When Patrick got home, he was relieved to find that Jack was out. He wasn't in the mood to hear about his younger brother's day working at the video store or his girlfriend, a Goth nightmare who accessorised with oversized safety pins, reminding him of an extra in a Tim Burton movie. Without Jack there to distract him, he would be able to work out a plan to break up with Susan. After running through his options, he nixed the idea of calling it quits over the phone. It seemed as cold to him as his mate who had broken up with his girlfriend by leaving a message on her answering machine. But every time he had tried to tell her that it was not going to work out between them,

Susan deliberately derailed the conversation so that they were talking about everything *but* their relationship.

Patrick punched in Susan's number. She had one of those phones where you could put in a ring tone specific to a particular caller. His was the theme song to the America police drama, *Hawaii Five-0*. Whenever he rang her, Susan acted as if he were a sailor come home from the sea after a six-month cruise. He didn't think he deserved such attention. Correction: he knew he didn't deserve it.

While Patrick listened to a recap of Susan's day at the tanning salon, he opened Annie's file containing a computer printout of the notes he had given to DC Updike. After each of Annie's statements, Molly had made a comment, including a direct quote from Annie that caught his attention: "It can't possibly be him [Dr. Goh] because he's just my height (approx. 163 cm/5'-4"). My attacker was taller than that." Molly's question: "Do we have any idea how tall the assailant was?"

Susan was still talking about a client who wanted to have her moles removed when he interrupted her. "Listen, I have to go. I took a case file home, and something just popped out at me."

"I didn't think you were allowed to do that," Susan said, and Patrick was surprised that something he had said about police work had actually stuck. "It was okay to take this particular file. I really do have to go, but, Susan, we have to talk. It would probably be best if we went out to a restaurant. So think about going someplace where we can have a real conversation. I'll ring you tomorrow, and we'll set up a time and place."

"If you have to go, I won't keep you," she said, hurrying him off the phone. He had no doubt she knew what he wanted to talk to her about.

After pushing "end call" on his mobile, Patrick pressed #6 to call Annie. "I know it's late, but I just thought of something. I'd really appreciate it if you would let me come by your flat." Silence. "My partner typed up all the notes for your file, and something jumped out at me. I promise after this I won't bother you."

"You're not bothering me. It's just that I don't like to think about it."

"This is important."

"All right then. Come ahead. Have you eaten?"

"No, I haven't, but I'm not hungry." When things started to click, Patrick had little interest in anything but the case, and things were definitely falling into place.

Chapter 15

When Patrick got to Annie's flat, the outside door was unlocked and the interior light was still a sixty-watt bulb, two of his suggestions having been ignored, and he felt a wave of frustration come over him. There were a few simple things people could do to protect themselves from a break-in, but they were either too lazy or ignorant to do them. But when Annie opened the door, he abandoned the lecture he had planned to give her. It didn't seem right to land on someone so beautiful.

After finishing a cup of tea Annie had waiting for him, Patrick asked if she had any idea how tall her assailant was.

"No. I never saw him. After I got out of the hospital, I phoned Mr. Walsh, the dog walker, to thank him for rescuing me, and he said my attacker had a slight build and was a fast runner."

"You said that when your assailant grabbed you, he pulled you against him and your head rested against his body. Correct?" Annie nodded. "Where on his body did your head rest?"

"I don't know. I hadn't thought about it."

"It will probably help if we recreate the assault." Annie shook her head vigorously. "I know this is unsettling, but please bear with me."

Patrick got behind Annie, gently pulling her by her pony tail until her head rested against his chest.

"No, that's not right. I think my head hit his chin." Patrick lowered his body so that her head was resting under his chin. "Yes, that's right. When he spoke to me, his chin was against my ear."

"That means your assailant was only a few inches taller than you. That's short for a man."

"Maybe he was Irish," Annie said, trying to lighten the mood. "You know, a race of little people."

"Or maybe *he* was a *she*," Patrick answered, ignoring the jest.

"You're not serious," Annie said and started to laugh. Patrick adopted his stoic look, the one he had used when in uniform talking to smart-arsed teenagers. "But that's preposterous. Why would a woman want to hurt me? I accidentally stepped on her yoga mat?"

"You still do that?"

Patrick didn't get yoga at all. Mad Marta had also taken yoga lessons and had provided a demonstration of her flexibility by putting her legs behind her head. He had asked her if there was any time in her life

137

when such a pose would be necessary? Her answer: If someone broke into her flat and she needed to hide, she could fit in a really small space. Another reason to say adios to Miss Bledsloe.

"Yes. I still do that—but at the council centre. I can't afford the health club any longer. But never mind that. What makes you think my attacker might be a woman."

"Her height, her build, the fact she was wearing an anorak. It wasn't that cold that night, but if she's trying to conceal her sex, the heavy coat makes sense. And then there's the cut on your face. That mark was made by a ring with a high setting, in other words, a woman's ring." Patrick traced the wound with his finger. "If it's a woman that changes everything."

"But it doesn't make sense," Annie said, inching closer to Patrick. "I haven't done anything to warrant a woman attacking me."

"Annie, these days, it doesn't take much to set someone off. You said you still go to dance clubs and the pub. Maybe you chatted up some bloke, and his girlfriend didn't like it. When I was in uniform, I saw it all the time. Little incidents leading to big fights," and he took her hands in his. "You're going to have to look at this assault in a completely different light. I want you to think about women you have known from work, university, dance clubs, pubs, yoga, etc."

After each suggestion, Annie shook her head, but

with Patrick holding her hands, she wasn't thinking straight.

"Annie, the fact is you got under someone's skin, and you need to look at it from that point of view. And there are other things you need to do as well. Let's start with locking the front door. Do you know how easy it would be for someone to hide in the stairwell and pounce when you came out of your flat? Do you have any idea how many women are sexually assaulted because they didn't...?"

"Yes. I understand. It would be an easy thing to do," she said, putting her fingers to his lips, allowing them to linger. "I promise that tomorrow I'll talk to Mr. Higgins about giving his daughters keys to the front door so we can keep it locked. He's a sweet man. He won't mind. He saw you working on the lock, and I told him you were a policeman who was looking after me so he wouldn't worry. But, please, no more, Patrick. I'm frightened enough as it is."

Seeing that she really was frightened, he took her in his arms and gave her a quick hug. Anything more would have to wait until he was no longer working the case. But with that brief contact, he knew he wanted to be with her again—had to be with her again.

"Give me a ring if you think of anything no matter how trivial," Patrick said, opening the door. "Let me decide what's important and make sure my number is in your phone list."

"It's already there." Despite their fifteen months of separation, she had never deleted it, and Patrick smiled at the thought. "And I'll do everything you have suggested, including asking your brother to trim the hedges, and I'll have Jack change out the light bulb in the stairwell while he's here."

Patrick gave Annie a quick peck on the cheek, but as soon as he set foot out on the landing, a body came hurling at him. After jumping on his back, his assailant was tearing at his hair and scratching his face. When she started screaming "Liar! Liar! You are such a bloody liar" in his ear, he realised it was Susan.

While Patrick attempted to shake her off, Annie pulled at her arms trying to break Susan's hold. Between the two of them, they were finally able to throw her to the floor. With Susan on her back and Patrick sitting on top of her, he was able to pin her arms above her head. The ruckus brought Mr. Higgins out of his ground-floor flat, and Annie yelled to him to call 999.

"Susan, stop! Please stop!" Patrick pleaded. "It's not what you think."

"You're a bloody liar," Susan said, continuing to flail. "I knew you were coming here. I knew it. You've been seeing her for weeks but didn't have the guts to tell me about it."

"Please calm down. We can talk about this."

"Get your god-damned arse off of me."

"I will if you promise to calm down." Slowly, he felt the fight go out of her. After Patrick was finally able to dismount, Susan crawled into a corner of the landing and started to cry.

"Annie, please get Susan a glass of water." After Annie went into the flat, Patrick sat down next to his now ex-girlfriend who looked completely shattered. "Susan, I wasn't lying to you. I was here because of Annie's assault. I told you the truth. I saw something in her file that I needed to talk to her about. If anything else was going on, I wouldn't be going home at 8:00, now would I?"

"You still love her, don't you?" Susan asked, her anguished face looking up at him. Patrick nodded. "You should have said."

"I know I should have. That's why I wanted to meet you for dinner tomorrow night—to tell you that it wasn't going to work out between you and me. I'm really sorry about this."

As Annie handed Susan the water, two uniformed policemen came bursting through the door and raced up the stairs, but Susan, now completely subdued, was sitting on the landing looking like a puppet without its strings. After helping her to her feet, Annie took her by the arm and led her into the flat, and the dejected figure took a seat on the couch.

Annie didn't think she had seen a more pathetic creature in her life.

After showing the constables his warrant card, Patrick explained what had happened.

"We received a 999 call that an officer was being assaulted."

Patrick shook his head. "This was not an assault—more like a really bad break up."

"Are you going to press charges, DS Shea?" PC Willis asked.

"Not about this, no," Patrick answered. "But two weeks ago, Annie Jameson, the other lady in the flat, was assaulted. We need to take Miss Corning in for questioning regarding that attack. I'd appreciate it if you could get things rolling at the nick, and I'll be along directly. But before you do, I want to talk to Susan."

After taking a seat next to her on the couch, Patrick explained that the constables would take her down to the station so she could make a statement. "I wish there was a way we could avoid this, but because a 999 call was made and officers responded, we have to go this route."

"Am I going to jail?"

"No. Definitely not for hitting me. But you will, however, need to be interviewed."

"By you?" she asked hopefully.

"No. I cannot conduct an interview for an incident in which I was involved. Don't worry about it. We'll get this sorted. But you can help by doing everything the constables tell you to do. It's for the best."

"I'm sorry, Patrick. I really am."

"No more than I am," he said, patting her hand. "I'll see you at the station."

After walking with Susan to the police car, Patrick returned to the flat to find Annie in tears.

"Boy, did I screw up," Patrick said, sitting next to her. "I've been trying to end it with Susan for weeks now. If I had succeeded, tonight would never have happened, and you wouldn't have been attacked."

"No one was really hurt—at least not tonight. Did you really have to arrest her?"

"She hasn't been arrested—not yet anyway. But that may change as it's highly probable it was Susan who assaulted you."

"She looked so pathetic sitting there—a lifeless doll," she said, tears streaming down her face. "Even if she was the one who attacked me, I won't press charges against her."

"It's not up to you any longer. Assault is a serious offence. If she committed the crime, then she'll be charged, but a statement from you will definitely help."

"What's going to happen to her tonight?"

"First, she will be interviewed at the Renwick nick, and I'll make sure she is treated well. What happens next will be determined by what she's says in the interview."

"Will I need to make a statement tonight?"

"Not tonight, but you will need to make a statement in the morning. We'll have it all sorted by then." After releasing her hand, he stood up. "Listen, I've got to go."

"Of course. You need to help Susan."

"I'll ring you as soon as I can. In the meantime, PC Willis will stay with you." Annie nodded at the woman police constable standing in the doorway.

"In that case, I had better put the kettle on."

Chapter 16

In a police station, there were few secrets. As soon as he walked through the doors of the Renwick nick, Patrick knew everyone had heard that DS Shea's girlfriend had been taken into custody in connection with the assault of said DS Shea. Because he had worked with these same men and women for years during his posting to Renwick, there would be no smug faces or smirks—at least not today. All the teasing was down the pike after everything had been sorted. There was also the knowledge that being a copper required balancing the needs of one's personal life with the demands of the job. Everyone knew of Patrick's work ethic: Everything and everyone, except his son, came second to the job. It seemed that #2 had staged a revolt.

"Who's doing the interview?" Patrick asked the desk sergeant.

"Rees and Battle."

Patrick nodded his head in approval. Sal Battle and Kathy Rees were experienced interviewers. Susan could not have done better.

"They haven't started yet," Sergeant Kane, the front desk officer, informed Patrick. "Miss Corning said she wouldn't answer any questions until she knew you were here. Says you know her better than anyone else and that you understand she would never hurt you."

"Too right."

Patrick was met in the hallway outside Interview Room 2 by Detective Inspector Rees. "Sorry about this, Patrick."

"Yeah. It's a bit of a mess, isn't it?"

"We have been informed that you do not intend to press charges, so what are we looking for in the interview?"

"I'm not interested in what happened tonight. It was a lover's quarrel that got out of hand. However, there is a possibility that Susan is the one who attacked Annie Jameson on December 2 on Old School Road. Although it's on Renwick's patch, because I knew Annie, I did some investigating on my own time."

"Has Miss Corning admitted to the assault?"

"No. I'm hoping for a confession. Has she asked for legal counsel?"

"No, not yet. Nor has she been cautioned. The officer who took her into custody said she was in such a state that it could be established later in court that she didn't understand what was being said to her.

We'll take care of that as soon as we get started."

After recording the date and time of the interview, DI Rees began. "Susan Corning, you do not have to say anything, but it may harm your defence if you do not mention, when questioned, something which you later rely on in court. Anything you do say may be given in evidence. Do you understand?"

"Yes, I've seen it on the telly. But I'm not going to court. Patrick said..."

"Cautioning you is standard procedure," DI Rees said, interrupting her. She did not want to leave Susan with the impression that DS Shea was the one who would determine her future. "It's important you understand your rights. Now, would you like to make a statement?"

"Yeah, I do, but is Patrick here?"

"DS Shea is observing the interview by video from another room."

"That's all right then. I'll tell you what happened."

After taking a drink of water, Susan started with a recap of their rocky romance.

"Patrick and I have been seeing each other for about four months. It was obvious from the beginning that I liked him more than he liked me, but we got along, and so I stayed with him hoping things might change. Things did change, but not for the better. About a week ago, he told me he wasn't coming

147

home because a friend of his was in hospital. He said her name was Annie Jameson and that she had been assaulted. I knew the name because Patrick's brother, Jack, told me that they had almost got married and that he was still in love with her."

Battle and Rees exchanged looks. "Yeah, I know. Jack is really immature—not like Patrick at all. It is unbelievable what comes out of his mouth. Anyway, because of the attack, I knew Annie was back in the picture, and that's when Patrick started making all these excuses for not coming home, I mean, to my flat. He doesn't like it when I say it's his home.

"I don't know why he liked Annie better than me. I did everything he wanted. I tried to be the best girlfriend I could, but he preferred a girl who cheated on him. Lately, it's been one excuse after another for why he wasn't coming over. But tonight, I had a surprise waiting for him. He's a real big fan of Humphry Bogart, so when I found a collection of Bogart's films at the video store, I thought it might make a difference if I pretended to like something he did. I even made his favourite dinner, a curry. But then he rang to tell me he wasn't coming because he had to work a case. I was pretty sure where he was going, and sure enough, when I got to Renwick, his car was down the street from where Annie lives, so I knew he was there."

"How did you know where Annie Jameson lives?" DI Rees asked in a soothing voice. The suspect looked as if she was about to unravel. When she wasn't biting her thumbs, she was twisting her hair or squirming in her chair.

"While he was asleep, I got her telephone number from Patrick's mobile, and then I looked up her address on the internet. It's really not hard. You can find out almost anything on the internet these days. Because the front door to her house wasn't locked, I walked right in and waited outside the door to her flat on the stairs going up to the attics. I was going to confront Patrick right then and there. You know, try to embarrass him in front of his lady. I wanted him to feel as bad as I was feeling. Just get it off my chest— nothing physical—but when he kissed her, I just lost it. And then it didn't seem but a minute before the police came. After that, I went into Annie's flat, and she made me a cup of tea."

"You said you could learn just about anything on the internet about a person. Would that include where Annie Jameson went to university?" DI Rees asked.

"I guess," Susan answered with a shrug.

"Were you aware that Annie was assaulted on December 2nd on Old School Road?"

"Yeah. I already said that. Patrick told me."

"At the time of the assault, were you aware that DS Shea had re-established contact with Annie Jameson?"

"Yeah, I did. I ran into an old girlfriend of his at

the market. We've become mates, and we talk on the phone every day. She said she wanted to warn me about Patrick, saying he had girls stashed all over London. I didn't believe her, so she told me about Annie."

"And that made you angry?"

"Well, it didn't make me happy. Things weren't going well as it was. I didn't need an old girlfriend showing up."

"You would have had reason to be angry with Annie Jameson. After all, there was a chance Patrick was going to leave you for her. Did you want to punish her for taking your boyfriend?"

"Punish her? Now wait a minute! What are you going on about?" Susan said, pushing her chair away from the table. "I never did anything to Annie. Tonight was the first time I ever laid eyes on her. Do you think I'm the one who hurt her? I swear I never did." A look of panic came over her, and Susan jumped out of her chair. "Patrick, tell them I would never do such a thing. I am not a violent person," she said, turning full circle in an attempt to address the unseen DS Shea.

When Susan had mentioned an "old girlfriend," an alarm bell had gone off in Patrick's head. Seeing Susan's complete panic when it was suggested it was she who had assaulted Annie, he knew she was telling the truth, and he raced to the interview room.

"Susan, what was the name of my old girlfriend, the one you met at the market, the one who told you I was seeing Annie?"

"Marta. I don't know her last name. She said you dumped her and then told lies about her."

"Inspector Rees, I believe Susan did not assault Annie Jameson, but I think I know who did. PC Willis is with Annie at her flat. Please ring her and tell her that the name of the person who assaulted Annie is Marta Bledsoe. She is unstable and potentially dangerous. Tell PC Willis and Annie I'm on my way over."

"We'll get a patrol car over there right away," DS Battle said and hurried down the hall to the police dispatcher.

As Patrick was going out the door of the station, Molly Updike was coming in. "I heard you hit a spot of strife."

"I can't talk now I have to get to Annie's."

"I'll drive," Molly said and steered Patrick in the direction of her car. "You ring Annie."

En route, Patrick fumbled with his mobile. Now that he knew Marta was involved, he was scared witless for Annie because he had first-hand experience with just how screwed up Marta Bledsloe was.

A few days after the conclusion of their brief relationship, and long past midnight, Patrick had left the station to find Marta waiting for him. Unsure of when his shift would end, she had been sitting in her car for two hours. Patrick didn't scare easily, but that had scared the shit out of him. Her stakeout at the Hampden nick had been followed by endless calls and sexually-explicit e-mails with accompanying photographs that one usually saw in a porn magazine. He finally snapped when he saw her Escort parked on the street outside his flat. The harassment had stopped only after he had threatened her with a non-molestation order.

"Damn, I hit the wrong number. Okay, calm down, Shea. Start all over. #6. It's ringing. Why isn't she answering?" he asked Molly. "Why isn't the constable answering?"

"Maybe she's in the loo?"

"What? Both of them?" Patrick could hear the fear in his voice. "Annie, it's Patrick. I need to speak to PC Willis."

"She's not here. I told her to go home."

"Why?"

"Because the person who attacked me is in police custody. It was a waste of her time to babysit me. She rang the station, and the desk sergeant said he'd let you know she was leaving."

"Really? You told a constable to go home? So glad you know more than I do. I've only been doing this for eight years."

"I don't understand why you are angry at *me*. Susan was after *you*."

"I'll tell you later. Right now, I need..."

"Hold on, Patrick. There's someone at the door. It's probably PC Willis." Patrick heard the sound of the phone being placed on the kitchen counter.

"Don't put the phone down!" Patrick screamed. But his shout was drowned out by the sound of a door being knocked in. He could also hear Annie's muffled protests and a scuffle, but then there was silence. The call had ended.

"Marta's there. She's broken into Annie's flat."

Chapter 17

By the time Patrick reached Annie's house, uniformed police had already arrived, and the nosy-neighbour crowd was gathering.

"I am DS Shea," Patrick said, showing his warrant card to the two uniformed policemen. "What's happening?" Patrick asked, his mouth so dry, he could barely get the words out.

"A woman broke into the upstairs flat and is holding a hostage inside. That's PC Kroll inside the front door, and PC Morton is on the landing. The door is hanging by one hinge, and so it's open enough so that Morton can see in. Both women are sitting on the couch, but the hostage taker is holding a kitchen knife."

"Okay, that's good if they're just sitting there. While I talk to PC Morton, I want you to get me a stab vest."

From the foot of the stairs, PC Morton was visible, and Patrick indicated that once he had his vest on he would be coming up. Through gestures, it was established that the two women remained on the couch with Marta holding a knife.

"The hostage taker's name is Marta Bledsloe," Patrick whispered. "I want you to tell Marta that Patrick Shea would like to speak to her."

"I'll do that, sir. She's been expecting you."

After being promoted to detective sergeant, Patrick had taken a course at the crime college in dealing with hostage situations. Now that he had to employ the techniques he had been taught, his mind was a muddle. But he did remember one thing: establish a rapport with the hostage taker. After putting on the vest, he stepped into view.

"Long time, no see, Patrick," Marta answered, her voice quavering. With her dark hair poking out every which way from a hairclip and her eyes blazing, she looked deranged.

"Hello, Patrick," Annie said. "Marta and I are having a chat."

"Chatting is good."

"I didn't want this," Marta said, showing him the knife. "I just wanted to talk to her about you. You know, warn her what you are really like. Did you know she's been following you around?"

"May I come in and sit down?"

"No, you're fine where you are," Marta answered, gesturing with the knife that he should stay near the door. "You didn't answer my question, Patrick. Did you know it was no coincidence that she ran into you at Tesco's? She knows you're a creature of habit. Twice a month, you draw out money from your account, and then you fill up your freezer with frozen pizzas and those little entrees and buy beer. You never miss—the fifteenth and the last day of the month. She knew that too. But what she didn't know was that if you found out she's been following you that you'd threaten her with a non-molestation order just like you did with me. That was a really cheap shot."

Patrick could hear the anger edging into Marta's voice. He would have felt better if she referred to Annie by name, indicating that a bond had been formed, but everything was "she." It would be best if he made the crisis his own.

"Yes, it was, Marta. I had had a long day, and it just came out. I'm very sorry about that because I know it hurt your feelings. I wish I could have a redo on that one."

"Oh, you say you're sorry, but I don't believe you," Marta answered, shaking her head. "You know why? Because you're a selfish bastard, that's why. After seeing you and her practically snogging in Tesco's, I thought I'd warn her about you. I already knew that after school she cut across the heath, so I waited for her on Old School Road. I really didn't mean to hurt her. But when I thought about how you threw me over, treating me like a piece of shit on the bottom of your shoe, I got so pissed off that I hit her. If she had only listened to me, I wouldn't have had to come here tonight."

"You wanted to hit me instead," Patrick said, trying to draw all her anger toward him.

"Marta, if I may say something?" Annie said, her voice surprisingly calm. Patrick shook his head to warn Annie off, but she ignored him. "You are wrong about Patrick and me. You see, Patrick broke up with me because he thinks I cheated on him in a one-night fling. Because of that, he told me he would never forgive me, and he hasn't. It's only because of the attack that we've been in each other's company, but we're just friends. I swear."

"Is that true, Patrick? You chucked her out because she cheated on you the one time." Patrick nodded. "Well, you really are a prick, aren't you? You don't deserve either of us."

"I can't disagree with that, and it's a bit of a mess, but we don't want it to get any messier," Patrick said, pointing to the knife. "Up to this point, everything is manageable, but if you don't put the knife down, things get more complicated."

"I know I need help."

"We can get you help."

"I don't want to go to prison."

"I don't think that will happen. But we can't get started until you put the knife down."

"All right then," and Marta tossed the knife on the floor. After picking up the weapon, Patrick motioned for the PC Morton to come in. Marta didn't struggle when the constable placed the cuffs on her and led her down the stairs. He advised PC Kroll to make sure that she had legal counsel. "She's mentally unstable, and she'll need proper representation."

"We'll see to it, sir."

When Patrick returned to Annie's flat, he tried to take her in his arms, but she pushed him away. "Where do you pick up your girlfriends? At an asylum?" And tears poured down her face.

"I'm so sorry," he said, and he gently pulled her toward him. "It's going to be all right. I promise. It will be all right. It's over."

* * *

After comforting Annie, Patrick told her that he had to go down to the station. "But you can't stay here," Patrick said, looking at the door clinging to the one hinge. "You can go back to my flat if you want." Annie nodded. "This is my partner, Molly Updike," Patrick said as the detective constable entered the room.

"Did I hear you're going back to Patrick's flat?" Annie again nodded. "I can drive you there, and we'll have a nice cup of tea."

"What about Eddie?" Patrick asked of Molly's

husband.

"He told me to do whatever was necessary. He knows you're my mate." Patrick smiled in appreciation.

"Patrick, I think I should go down to the police station and make a statement," Annie said. "Things weren't as dire as they looked. I never thought Marta would actually stab me."

"I understand, but Marta's going to need legal counsel, and it could take hours for her brief or a duty solicitor to get there. So get a good night's sleep, and we'll take your statements about both incidents in the morning."

"We have to talk, Patrick," Annie said, placing her hand on his sleeve. "Tonight, things were said that weren't true."

"Yes, we have to talk," and he placed his hand on her cheek. "I'd like to start by saying how sorry I am that this happened to you."

Annie shook her head. "This whole thing is actually my fault."

"We can argue about who's more at fault when I get back."

"I think this time, I'll win."

Chapter 18

As Patrick exited Annie's house, he was met by a crowd of on-lookers and reporters from a TV station and Patricia Gresham from *Global News*. Hoping for an interview, Gresham had cornered Superintendent Anita Lawrence from the Renwick station. Seeing his former boss confirmed that this incident had blown up in his face, and with it, any hope of his being assigned to New Scotland Yard.

As soon as Gresham saw Patrick, she shouted out his name and waved and gestured with her notepad for him to join her, but Patrick shook his head and went back into the building to warn Annie of the circus that awaited her.

"I'll be fine unless you think another one of your old girlfriends is out there waiting," Annie said, trying to lighten the mood, but Patrick winced at her comment.

"I'm fresh out of girlfriends," he said. "But, seriously, do you really think the press is going to go away? In the morning, you'll find them hiding in the shrubbery."

"They can hide all they want. I won't be here. I'm going to sneak out the back door and cut through the garden. I'll be staying with Molly for the next few days."

Molly nodded and said that it had been her idea. "Just because there's a circus out there, doesn't mean we have to feed the animals. I'm going to park my car on the street behind us, and PC Morton can walk Annie to the car. Too bad you can't make an escape as well," she said, placing her hand on her partner's shoulder.

"Make sure PC Morton uses a torch because it's a minefield back there. I hope he's up-to-date on his tetanus shots." After his poor attempt at humour, he closed his eyes and shook his head. "What a freaking nightmare!"

"Don't look so down in the dumps," Molly said. "It's not as bad as you think. You were in the newspaper today—picture and everything. You're the copper who nicked the Hampden Burglar."

* * *

When Patrick again stepped outside, he was met by floodlights from TV cameras and shouted questions from a bevy of television reporters who had joined Patricia Gresham. Ignoring all of them, he approached Superintendent Lawrence who was now standing inside the police tape with her back to the media.

"You've had a rough night of it, haven't you, Patrick?" she asked after handing him a cup of hot coffee poured from her Thermos.

"I'm sorry about all this, Guv. There was no need for you to come out."

"When I receive a call that an officer had been assaulted, I respond," she said. "I was on my way here when I got a second message saying the situation had been resolved and no officer was hurt. Because I was already in the car, I thought I'd come ahead. Then the third call came in: a possible hostage situation."

"I don't know that it ever was a hostage situation."

"Well, we'll find out during the interview. Care to ride back to the station with me?"

Patrick was a great admirer of Anita Lawrence, his super at the Renwick station, and someone whose door was always open to the men and women serving under her. She had come up through the ranks at a time when women were not warmly received in the Metropolitan Police. After each promotion, roadblocks had been put up to impede her progress, but the only way she could impress upon her male colleagues that she could do the job was to keep her cool. There was very little that could ruffle this bird's feathers, except a call that a fellow officer might be in harm's way.

"Why don't we take it from the top," Lawrence said as soon as they were in the car. "I want to hear your side of the story before the suspect is interviewed."

Too embarrassed to look her in the face, Patrick leaned back and stared straight ahead.

"Back in May, I met Marta Bledsloe at a dance club, and I went home with her, a bedsit on Hagen Road. Three days later I saw her again at her flat. We didn't go out," Patrick said, his face flaming at his admission of sex on the run. "Because I knew I wasn't going to see her again, when I was leaving, I told Marta I'd see her around. I had no idea how prophetic that statement would be.

"After I kept running into her all over the place, I realised she was following me, so I checked to see if we had anything in the computer on her. Although she was never charged, she was taken into custody twice for breach of peace after getting into a shoving match with two women in The Rogue, a pub in Renwick. Both times, she claimed these women were moving in on her boyfriend.

"After I read the reports, I knew I would have to take a more direct approach. Next time we bumped into each other, I told her I was not going to see her again. I blamed the job, long hours, etc., and so she decided to check it out. One night, I was on the late shift, and I didn't finish until after 1:00 in the morning. This was shortly after the thugs set fire to four cars in Hampden Commons. When I came out, I saw her sitting in her car waiting. A week later, it was the same thing, except this time she was outside my flat. That just did it for me. I told her that what she was doing was a form of harassment, and if she didn't stop, I would get a non-molestation order."

"Her reaction?"

"She let out a string of expletives and then drove off. I didn't see her again after that. But, apparently, she's been following me as well as Annie Jameson and Susan Corning. She's been a very busy woman."

"Well, she's obviously also a troubled woman. If she hasn't already asked for a brief, we'll get the duty solicitor to sit in on the interview. In fact, I'm going to take care of that right now." Lawrence rang the station telling them to have Kendall Garrett come in.

"Good news," Lawrence said, collapsing her phone. "Kendall is already there. They had him come in because the incident with Susan Corning involved a police officer."

"Who's going to do the interview with Marta?"

"I am."

Patrick stared out the window. He could almost hear a flushing sound as his career went down the toilet.

"Don't look so glum, Patrick. I know you were hoping for Scotland Yard, and it's still within the realm of the possible. Remember, you are the man who nicked the Hampden Burglar, and you got a quick resolution on the missing Dorsett girl." Patrick looked puzzled. How would a super from another station know about something so run-of-the-mill as recovering a runaway? "But it may require that you lay low for a while. If you'd like, I can have a talk with Superintendent Craig," his boss and the man responsible for putting together Patrick's file for submission to the review board.

Patrick laughed. "You know Craig. He plays it straight. This is as bent it comes."

When Patrick and Lawrence arrived at the station, they were informed by the desk sergeant that Susan Corning had made a statement and that she had been released without being charged and that a friend had taken her home. He indicated that the duty solicitor was still in the station.

"One down, one to go," Patrick mumbled to himself.

"As for the other young lady, Miss Bledsloe said she wants to make a statement and waives her right to counsel. She's in Room 1."

"Very good, Sergeant, but I still want the duty solicitor to sit in on this. And, Patrick, if you want to observe the interview from the video room, that's fine."

Patrick was soon joined by John Stanley.

Someone from Renwick had telephoned him to let him know that DS Shea was in a tight spot. With Molly, Lawrence, and now John Stanley having his back, Patrick felt better. He understood that once things settled down, he would be in for some unmerciful kidding, but for now, the troops were rallying behind him.

Like Susan Corning before her, Marta was prepared to make a full statement without benefit of counsel. However, Superintendent Lawrence, who was already looking ahead to how the Crown Prosecution Service would handle the case, encouraged her to use the services of the duty solicitor. Marta, who knew she was in deep shit, agreed.

Before the solicitor could sit down, Marta started talking, eager to discuss the knife.

"Miss Bledsloe, it would be best if we start at the beginning," Lawrence advised her, and after she was cautioned, Marta made a series of admissions, including witnessing Patrick's meeting with Annie Jameson at Tesco's, punching Annie in the head on Old School Road, approaching Susan Corning for the purpose of informing her that Shea was seeing Jameson, and following Shea to Jameson's flat.

"I was sitting in my car outside Annie's flat when all hell broke loose," Marta said in a calm voice, as if someone else's match had started the fire.

"But how did you know Susan Corning would go to Annie Jameson's flat tonight?" Lawrence asked.

"After I saw Patrick go into Annie's house, I rang Susan and told her that I had seen his car on Pullman Crescent, and I thought that might get a rise out of her. Well, it did. But when I saw the police cars pull up, I thought Susan must have killed Patrick, but then he came out and walked with her to the panda car. And I thought, that bastard got away with it again. After the woman police officer left, I went upstairs to talk to Annie, like I said, to warn her.

"But after taking one look at me, she tried to slam the door in my face. I didn't do anything to deserve that, so I rammed my shoulder into the door. One of the hinges gave way, and it flew open, knocking her down. I told her I just wanted to talk, but she ran for the phone. I reckoned she would ring the police, so I needed to do something to stop her. There was a knife on the cutting board, so I just picked it up to get her attention. I wasn't going to hurt her. I just wanted to talk, and we sat down on the couch. That's all we did—just talk. I never threatened to use the knife. I just wanted to tell her that Patrick wasn't worth it and that she shouldn't try to get back with him. But then the police came, and I knew I was in trouble. But I swear I would never have hurt her."

When the interview was over, Patrick gave his own statement and asked Lawrence what she thought the charges against Marta would be.

"First, we'll have to get Annie Jameson's statement. After all, Marta did knock her down when she broke into the flat, and with a knife present, there was the threat of violence. There is also the matter of the initial assault. However, considering Marta's mental state, I can imagine CPS allowing her to plead to a lesser charge as long as she agrees to counselling and supervision. But it's best not to speculate. You know how the Crown Prosecution Service is. They want watertight cases."

While straightening the papers in the file, Lawrence again offered to speak with Superintendent Craig on Patrick's behalf. "These events were precipitated by Marta Bledsoe's actions, not yours."

"Thanks, Guv, but, no thanks. It will look like I ran home to my mum, but I appreciate the offer."

"Well, since we are speaking of mothers, and I'm very near old enough to be yours, a word of advice. It is never a good idea to go home with a stranger no matter how enticing the offer."

"I know all this makes me look like a bloody hound, but I'm not. That line about me having women stashed all over London is bollocks. Excuse me, not true. When I met Marta, it had been six months since my split from Annie, and I hadn't been with anyone else. And, yes, I did want sex. But I didn't sneak out on Marta in the middle of the night. I took proper leave of her. It might have been better if I hadn't. But

I do have one question. Why did Marta get so upset about Annie and not Susan? Did she say?"

"Yes, as a matter of fact she did say something to PC Willis. Apparently, Marta didn't feel threatened by your relationship with Susan because it was obvious that you weren't in love with Susan Corning. However, Annie was another story. Apparently, your body language spoke volumes. So what's going to happen between you and Annie?"

"I don't know. Why would she want any part of me when I brought all this down on her head?"

"That may be true, but make sure you ask Annie what she thinks. You are not very good at guessing what women will do."

"Guilty," Patrick said. "That's why I have Molly Updike as a partner. She straightens me out. Speaking of Molly, she's with Annie. May I go?"

"Yes, but please see that Annie comes in tomorrow morning to make a statement. Because these incidents involved a police officer, I'll be the one to meet with CPS. After we get everything sorted, you might want to take a few days off. These things can really wear you out."

* * *

Patrick found Annie in Molly's lounge swaddled in blankets and surrounded by tea cups and tissues. Although she was no longer shedding tears, there was enough evidence present to know that she had had a good cry. The first words out of her mouth were to ask about Susan Corning. After hearing that Susan had been released, Annie relaxed. As far as Marta was concerned, she hoped the woman would receive the necessary treatment as she obviously had serious mental issues, but more than that, she hoped never to lay eyes on her again.

"First, I want to clear something up," Annie said after gesturing for Patrick to take a seat beside her on the couch. After stating that their meeting at the cashpoint machine had been entirely accidental, she admitted the second encounter in Tesco's had been planned. "After talking to you, even for that short period of time, I realised how much I missed you, and so I went back with the intention of *accidentally* bumping into you again. But after our chat at the market, I thought, Annie, get a grip. Patrick will never forgive you for what he thinks you did, so move on."

"What I *think* you did? What does that mean?"

Annie knew there was no way she was going to get through this without crying, and she reached for a box of tissues. "I never cheated on you. There was no one-night stand. I made it all up."

Patrick, with mouth agape, stared at her.

Annie explained how it had all come about. While still at Renwick, Patrick had been part of a team investigating rival gangs fighting over territory for distribution of narcotics on the Borders housing estate, an estate so crime ridden and dilapidated that it had since been torn down. Throughout the summer, tension between the two gangs had escalated. The denouement had been an exchange of gunfire between the warring gangs with a policeman shot in the leg and a drug dealer in hospital on life support. The incident had been the spark for a riot requiring every available policeman from the Renwick nick to go to the scene. Photographs and video of the shootout had ended up on the front pages of every newspaper and on all the evening newscasts. Annie knew that among the police officers assembled to quash the riot was Patrick Shea.

Although Patrick made light of it, Annie had been terribly frightened for him, and all his attempts to downplay the dangers policemen, including detectives, faced on a daily basis had failed to reassure her.

"I wanted to tell you the truth, but I knew what would happen. You'd lay on the charm, and then you'd tell me how driving to work is more dangerous than being a policeman. I'd heard it all before. But I couldn't shake the images of the Borders riot, and I thought I had to end it—for my sanity and because you needed someone who would support your career goals. That's when I made up that story about my fling. I knew if you thought I had cheated on you that you would break up with me, and you did. It was the biggest mistake of my life. I've missed you terribly."

Patrick sunk back into the couch. "Blimey" was all he could manage.

"I wish I could tell you that my feelings about your chosen profession have changed, but considering what happened tonight, that too would be a lie. What I can tell you is that I have never stopped loving you, and that the pain of being separated from you is greater than my fear of being in love with a copper."

"I'm not sure I'm following what you're saying."

"What I am trying to say is that I would like to give it another try, that is, if you can forgive me for lying to you."

"We all make mistakes, or so I've been told about a dozen times this week. I think I proved it tonight." Patrick felt tears forming and tried to keep them from running down his face. The last time he had cried was the night he had walked out on Annie. "I want you back, Annie. In the worst way, I want you back."

Annie fell into his arms, and for the first time in fifteen months, Patrick kissed a woman he was in love with, and it was even better than he had remembered. It wasn't but a minute before he could feel every inch of him responding to her touch, and she was having the same reaction because she was trying to open his shirt. As much as he wanted to make love to her, he didn't want Molly's son bursting in and getting a lesson in sex education.

"Colin is already in bed," Annie said, continuing to unbutton Patrick's shirt, "and it was Molly who mentioned that this is a sleeper sofa and gave me an extra pillow in case I had a visitor."

Patrick stood up, pulling Annie with him. "What are we waiting for? Help me get these cushions off."

After they made love, Patrick got out of bed and sat in a chair so that he could look at Annie while she lay sleeping. She was on her side, and with only the light from a street lamp filtering into the room, he traced the outline of her body: head, neck, shoulders, hips, and long legs. In the months since their breakup, he had performed this exercise so many times. It was as if her image had been burned on his retinas. But now it was no longer imagery. The feel of her skin, the taste of her lips, the exquisite feeling of being inside her—all real.

Annie sat up, and after her eyes adjusted to the dark, she found Patrick and patted the empty space next to her, and he went to her.

"I wanted you so badly that I'm afraid I rushed you a bit," Annie said, and Patrick laughed. His need for her had been so great that he had practically devoured her, and in the frenzy, he had come quickly. "I suggest we have another go. This time slower."

Patrick pushed Annie on her back, and before she had even touched him, he was ready to enter her. This time would probably be just as quick, but after so long a separation, he needed to reclaim her, and short and sweet made for a good start.

Chapter 19

Patrick was sitting in a chair opposite to Superintendent Craig waiting to hear the fallout from the Corning and Bledsloe incidents and wondering if his conduct would result in his being interviewed by Complaints and Disciplines. If found guilty of questionable conduct, instead of the hoped-for transfer to Scotland Yard, he might be demoted to detective constable, or worse, he would be back in uniform. But for Patrick, there was no going back to uniformed policing, and it looked as if he might end up being a plumber after all. At least, Annie would be happy about that.

"I've been reviewing your file, Patrick, and I have to say that the incidents involving the two women came at a bad time for you. After all, you were our shiny penny, what with you being the one who captured the Hampden Burglar and recovered Tanya Dorsett. There was also the cold case I gave you that you handled quite well. I had a letter from Mrs. Langford complimenting both you and DC Updike."

Patrick thought what a load of shit. He hadn't "captured" the Hampden Burglar; Jacobs had surrendered without a fight. As far as Tanya Dorsett was concerned, all he had done was routine police work, in cooperation with two uniformed cops, in "recovering" someone who was eager to be found, and the Langford case should never have been reopened. He was being praised as a stellar copper for providing basic police services, but if it meant he would remain a detective sergeant, he would keep his mouth shut.

"There were no charges made against Miss Corning," Craig continued. "As far as Miss Bledsloe is concerned, her future is in the hands of the Crown Prosecution Service. If there is a trial, you will have to testify, but that could be a ways down the road. There's nothing to be gained by speculating what CPS will do.

"In speaking with Superintendent Lawrence about all this, she informed me that your relationship with Miss Bledsloe was little more than gratuitous sex, but there is a lesson to be learnt there. As I tell my children, sex is a lot more complicated than an exchange of body fluids. Each time you engage in intercourse, you give a little bit of yourself away, and it can come back to haunt you."

Patrick looked down at his hands, trying not to laugh. He felt as if he was back in his sex education class in secondary school.

"Lesson learnt, sir. I can assure you of that."

"Just a little bit of fatherly advice there." Patrick waited for additional pearls of wisdom to fall from Craig's lips. "Because I do think of my younger officers very much as my lads—and lasses," he said, laughing. "We mustn't forget the ladies."

"No, sir."

"But I won't be in a position to give you this advice for much longer..."

So he wasn't off the hook, Patrick thought. There would be consequences after all.

"...because, my boy, you are going to New Scotland Yard, effective January 9."

"You're not having me on, are you, sir?" Patrick asked stunned by Craig's statement.

"No, Patrick, I am not having you on. I'm not the only one who has noticed your talent as a detective sergeant. You received letters of recommendation in recognition of your excellent service to the Renwick and Hampden stations. In fact, I think it was Superintendent Lawrence's letter that sealed the deal. I had the privilege of putting your file together with my own recommendation that you be assigned to Scotland Yard and a murder investigation team. Of course, what actually happens once you get to the Yard is not up to me. You may end up inputting data on a computer for all I know. And it's a good time to start as 2004 marks the 175th anniversary of Scotland Yard. But that's neither here nor there. May I be the first to offer my congratulations?"

Patrick didn't know what to say. It had been a life-long dream to work at the Yard, and now that it had finally arrived, he was speechless.

"I had exactly the same reaction when I was notified of my promotion to superintendent. But when it finally dawned on me that this was the real deal, I telephoned my wife. Is there someone special you would like to ring?"

"Yes, sir. Someone very special." He thought of Annie.

THE END

Glossary of British Terms

Brief – A lawyer, especially a barrister

Bedsit – A furnished sitting room containing sleeping accommodations and sometimes cooking and washing facilities

BMW – Although BMW is considered a luxury car in the U.S., in Britain, they are used as police cars.

CID – Criminal Investigation Department is the branch of all Territorial police forces within the British Police to which plain-clothes detectives belong. CID officers are involved in investigation of major crimes such as rape, murder, serious assault, and fraud.

CPS – The Crown Prosecution Service is a non-ministerial department of the United Kingdom government responsible for public prosecutions of people charged with criminal offences in England and Wales. The CPS is responsible for criminal cases beyond the investigation, which is the role of the police. This involves giving advice to the police on charges to bring, being responsible for authorising all but a very few simple charges, and preparing and presenting cases for court, both in magistrates' courts and the Crown court.

First floor – In the United States, this would be the second floor. The entry level is on the ground floor in the United Kingdom. The floor above it is the first floor.

Form – Having a criminal record

Hendon – Hendon Police College is the principal training centre for the London Metropolitan Police Service. The college is today officially called the Peel Centre. Within the police service, it is known as "Hendon."

Housing Estate – Equivalent to the Projects in the U.S.

Metropolitan Police Service (the Met) – MPS is the territorial police force responsible for Greater London, excluding the "square mile" of the City of London, which is the responsibility of the City of London Police.

Nick – A police station

New Scotland Yard – The Yard is the headquarters of the Metropolitan Police Service in London. It derives its name from the location of the original Metropolitan Police headquarters at 4 Whitehall Place that had a rear entrance on a street called Great Scotland Yard. The Scotland Yard entrance became the public entrance to the police station. Over time, the street and the Metropolitan Police became synonymous.

Non-molestation order – A restraining order

Police ranks in the Metropolitan Police: Police constable (PC), detective constable (DC), sergeant, detective sergeant (DS), detective inspector (DI), detective chief inspector (DCI), superintendent, chief superintendent, commander, deputy assistant commissioner, assistant commissioner, deputy commissioner, and commissioner.

Snout – An informant

Squat – An abandoned property inhabited by the homeless

NOW AVAILABLE

A Killing in Kensington

Detective Sergeant Patrick Shea of London's Metropolitan Police and his new partner, Detective Inspector Tommy Boyle, have been handed a high-profile murder case. In the penthouse of Kensington Tower, womaniser Clifton Trentmore, President of Trentmore World Imports, lay dead with his head bashed in. The investigation reveals a man who was loathed by both sexes. With too few clues and too many suspects, Shea must determine who hated Trentmore enough to kill him. But as Patrick digs deeper, he finds his suspects have secrets of their own.

A Death in Hampden

When pop rock star, Derek Prince, is found dead in his London mansion, the case is given to Detective Chief Inspector Tommy Boyle and his sergeant, DS Patrick Shea, of New Scotland Yard. Although Prince's ex-girlfriend, Chloe Hastert, was found walking Hampden's High Street drenched in the singer's blood and carrying the knife that killed him, there is something about the case that doesn't sit right with DS Shea. But with everyone believing the killer is already in custody and pressure to close the case, it falls to the two detectives to make sure they have got it right.

Acknowledgements

I would like to thank Paul, Nancy, Kathe, Sally, Carole, Candy, Susan, Jakki, and Mark for their suggestions and support. I am especially indebted to fellow author, Karen Aminadra, a friend in the UK, for reviewing the manuscript in an effort to ferret out any Americanisms.

Other books by Mary Lydon Simonsen:

From Sourcebooks:
Searching for Pemberley
The Perfect Bride for Mr. Darcy
A Wife for Mr. Darcy
Mr. Darcy's Bite

From Quail Creek Crossing:
Novels:
Darcy Goes to War
Darcy on the Hudson
Becoming Elizabeth Darcy

Novellas:
For All the Wrong Reasons
Captain Wentworth Home from the Sea
Mr. Darcy's Angel of Mercy
A Walk in the Meadows at Rosings Park
Mr. Darcy Bites Back

Short Story:
Darcy and Elizabeth: The Language of the Fan

Modern Novel:
The Second Date: Love Italian-American Style

Patrick Shea Mystery:
A Killing in Kensington

27634558R00113

Made in the USA
Lexington, KY
17 November 2013